Triple Shot

A Last Call Crime Club Mystery

KC Walker

Copyright © 2025 by KC Walker

All rights reserved.

Published by Laragray Press

No part of this book may be reproduced in any form or by any electronic or mechanical means without written permission from the author, except for the use of brief quotations in a book review.

This is a work of fiction. All names, characters, locales, and incidents are products of the author's imagination and any resemblance to actual people, places, or events is coincidental except for the author's rescue dog Kit.

For more information about me and all my books or to contact me, visit www.kcwalkerauthor.com and sign up for updates about me and the real Kit.

Mariah Sinclair designed my stunning and delightful cover. You can find her at https://www.thecovervault.com.

I'm so grateful to all my author friends and acquaintances who have offered support, community, and laughs throughout the past several years. My life is so much richer with all of you in it.

A special acknowledgement to my readers, reviewers, beta readers, typo-catchers, and those of you who send me emails of encouragement and story ideas. You mean the world to me!

Chapter One

Years of stunt work had sharpened my instincts, and as I stepped out into the frigid morning, they whispered a warning. Too bad I wasn't listening. I had cinnamon rolls on my mind, the sort that made you forget your troubles—at least for a few gooey minutes.

My grandmother, Bobbie, called out to me from the end of the driveway. "Whitley Leland, what is taking you so long?"

"We're not taking the car?" I asked, hoping the use of my full name didn't mean I was in trouble.

"The weather's finally warming up. A walk will do us good."

She led Kit and me down the icy street, the three of us dressed in matching bright red puffer coats. Kit's jacket came with matching booties, but the little mutt refused to wear them, so I tucked her under my arm.

How anyone thought below-freezing temperatures meant the weather was "warming up" was beyond me. As we reached the shopping district, the streets were deserted. Apparently, everyone else in town had the good sense to stay indoors.

We split up the errands, and since they wouldn't let dogs inside the General Store, Kit went with Bobbie. Of course I finished my shopping first. If Bobbie had found a friend with gossip, I'd be in for a long wait.

With my backpack heavy with the essentials of life—milk, sugar, and coffee—I paced the sidewalk, impatient to get to Sugarbuns Bakery for a warm cinnamon roll.

A black limousine, a rare sight in our small town, pulled up to the curb. The rear window slowly rolled down, like in a scene from a mafia movie. A woman with the same brown hair, eyes, and skin as mine eyed me with cool detachment. Anyone could have seen the family resemblance, except for the stark difference in presentation—her flawless makeup and sleek ponytail were worlds apart from my bare face and short-cropped hair.

I took a few steps closer. "Hello, Aunt Isabella." That was a mouthful. "How about Aunt Izzy?"

"Please do not call me that." Her voice, as smooth and sweet as Sugarbuns' rolls, held an edge. "Why don't you hop in the car, and we can talk privately."

"I'm kinda busy." Even though I had no doubt that this woman I'd only met a few days earlier was my aunt, I didn't trust her for a moment.

"I can tell you all about your father if you'd like. You must be curious."

Curious? Heck, yeah. I'd never met my father and had no memory of my birth mother. I was still an infant when Julia signed papers for me to be adopted by her brother and his wife. In nearly thirty years, Julia never bothered to send me so much as a postcard.

"Maybe another time." I reached in my pocket to wrap my hand around the locket that Isabella had given me. Julia's locket. It held a picture of Isabella's brother, Alejandro. It was the first picture I'd ever seen of my birth father.

"I have no idea when I might be back, Whitley. Do you really want to miss this opportunity?"

If we were shooting a movie, some burly guy would jump out and attempt to force me into the car. After some cool moves on my part, including flipping the guy over my shoulder, I'd lead them on a chase through the city. Fun times. But this was real life, and I had a decision to make.

Sensing my reluctance, Isabella gave me a brilliant movie star smile. "No funny business. I promise."

She pushed the door open and slid across the seat, gesturing for me to join her. Against my better judgment, I took a step closer just as a gunshot whizzed right past my left ear.

Isabella's composed face contorted in shock as she slammed the door shut. I dove to the ground as the limo peeled away, tires squealing. Two more shots rang out, and one pinged as it hit the limo.

"Thanks for the backup, Isabella," I grumbled with my cheek pressed against the icy pavement. I barely dared to breathe, remaining flat on the ground in case the shooter wanted to try again. The shots had come from across the street, possibly from the narrow driveway between the hardware store and the dry cleaners.

Movement caught my eye. False alarm—just a cat sauntering along without a care in the world. If anyone had been in the driveway, they were long gone now. But what if they weren't? I lay still just in case and peered up and down the still deserted street.

I recognized the pair of sensible, black lace-up shoes that appeared next to me along with Kit, who licked my cheek.

"Were those shots I heard?" my grandmother asked, her voice tinged with worry.

In one move, I was on my feet. I grabbed Bobbie by the arm and made a beeline for the nearest café as she tugged Kit along behind her.

"Three gunshots," I breathlessly explained, urging Bobbie through the café's front door into a tiny vestibule. When we went through the second door, a low growl came from Kit as I scanned the room. At least a dozen cats fixed their eyes on us, some wide with alarm, others half-lidded with mild interest. A calico with a torn ear watched us with the intensity of a guard on patrol.

"What kind of café is this?" I asked Bobbie.

"It's a cat café," she said, pulling her phone from her purse. "I'll call the police. I have a few questions for you before they arrive."

Kit's growl deepened as an oversized, fluffy, gray tabby crept closer with its curious eyes locked on us. Before I could react, Kit's warning became a sharp bark as she lunged, jerking at the leash and sending the startled tabby yowling and fleeing in a blur of fur.

As I scooped up the dog, a plump woman in an oversized sweatshirt with the words, "Catnip made me do it," rushed over, flapping her arms in alarm. Her salt-and-pepper curls bounced with each step as she cried out, "No dogs allowed!"

Bobbie spoke in a calm, soothing voice. "It's alright, Mrs. Nettle. We just needed a safe place to wait for the police."

"The police?" The woman's jaw went slack. I wondered if all her permits were up to date.

"Didn't you hear the shots outside?"

"I thought it must be a car backfiring. Are you saying—?" She swallowed hard. "Are we in danger?"

Bobbie peered out the window. "The shooter is long gone by now, I'm sure."

The woman placed her hand on her chest. "Oh, my. Mrs. Leland, you really shouldn't scare me like that. I've been managing my blood pressure through diet and prescription medication, and I've started doing yoga, but at my age..."

"At your age?" Bobbie scoffed. "Wait until you hit your seventies!"

"Bobbie," I interrupted, hoping to get her back on track. "You were going to call the police?"

While she made the call, I held Kit firmly as several brave cats approached us. My little mutt's lip curled, but she didn't make a peep, seemingly intimidated into silence. Since it seemed we were stuck there for a while, I plopped down in a chair facing the door.

Bobbie hung up and tried to reassure Mrs. Nettle. "As soon as the police arrive, we'll get out of your hair."

"Oh..." Her eyes darted around the room at her cats, most of whom seemed to have recovered from the excitement of having a dog enter their space. She sighed loudly.

"Can I get you something? A Cat-puccino or Kit-tea, perhaps?"

"Kitty?" I asked. "To drink?"

When she repeated the drink name more slowly, Kit's ears briefly perked up at the sound of her name. With all the cat hair floating around, I wasn't about to drink anything she gave me unless it came in a sealed bottle.

"Or," Mrs. Nettle said hopefully, "if you're hungry, I just baked a batch of Tabby Tarts."

Bobbie answered for both of us. "Nothing right now, thank you."

While we waited, I gave Bobbie the short version of what had happened, ignoring her raised eyebrows when I told her about meeting my birth dad's sister.

"Isabella is a piece of work—not used to anyone telling her no. I'm pretty sure the shots were aimed at her limo, although that first one came pretty close to me." Did the shooter have a bad aim, or... "I think they purposely missed me. Isabella too."

"Why shoot at you if they don't want to...?"

"Kill me?" I shuddered. "This is getting a little too real."

Chapter Two

"I don't like it," Bobbie said. "I don't like it at all."

"I don't like being shot at either, trust me." I shooed away a Siamese cat whose pale blue eyes were locked on Kit.

"Next time your aunt contacts you, would you tell me when it happens instead of waiting?"

Before I could decide how to answer that, Deputy Wallenthorp entered the café, followed by another officer. After taking my statement, they went back outside.

"They'll be looking for shell casings from the firearm." Bobbie loved sharing what she'd learned from her private investigator classes with me whether I wanted to listen or not. "Although revolvers retain the spent casings inside the cylinder. There should be some slugs from where the bullets landed, maybe in the wall of one of the shops across the street."

Twenty minutes or so later, Wallenthorp returned, his

lips curling in a smirk. "We've found no evidence of a shooting."

"Yet, you mean," I said. "You haven't found anything *yet*."

Wallenthorp grunted. "The department has limited resources. We can't waste time on frivolous reports."

"Frivolous?" I jumped to my feet, dropping Kit onto the ground. Startled, she barked and lunged at Wallenthorp, who jumped back a good foot. I would have laughed if I hadn't been so angry.

"We will expect a thorough investigation," Bobbie said. "Or the mayor will hear about it."

The deputy scowled. "Are you threatening me?"

"If telling someone to do their job is threatening, then yes."

Wallenthorp's face reddened as he sputtered. "We'll see about that." He turned and stormed out of the café.

As soon as he left, Bobbie got on the phone with her partner at Arrow Investigations. Bernard Fernsby had taken her on as an intern and investor with the intention of buying him out after she got her license, if they both lived that long.

"Bernard will do his own investigation and report back." Bobbie asked if I'd like a Cat-puccino, but I had a better idea.

"Let's go to Sugarbuns." I needed some comfort food after being fired at. I wouldn't say no to a shot of whiskey to settle my nerves, although I might have to settle for a latte, preferably one without cat hair.

As we walked the short distance to the bakery, I felt

exposed on the sidewalk. My pulse quickened every time a car passed by.

Meanwhile, Bobbie continued to grill me. "Why didn't you tell me about meeting your aunt?"

I replied with a question of my own. "Why didn't you tell me that you'd heard from Julia?"

"If your mother found out I told you anything about Julia, she'd kill me."

By "mother," Bobbie meant Angela, my adoptive mother, who was also my aunt by marriage. I suspected it was Angela's need for control rather than motherly love that motivated all the secret keeping.

We'd arrived at Sugarbuns, so I put a temporary hold on the conversation. "We can talk later."

The door jingled as we stepped inside, and Mitsy looked up from the counter, a grin spreading across her rosy-cheeked face. "Hey, Whit!" In a flash, she came from behind the bakery cases and crouched down in front of Kit, whose fluffy tail dusted the spotless floors.

"Where have you been, you little cutie pie?" Mitsy asked Kit in a sing-song voice scratching the little mutt's ears.

Bobbie elbowed me, and I turned to her to ask, "You've never been to Sugarbuns?"

"Of course I have, but we've never been formally introduced."

"Gosh. We'll have to fix that right away." A sarcastic note might have slipped into my voice. "Mitsy. May I present my grandmother, Bobbie. Bobbie, this is Mitsy."

Mitsy grinned. "Nice to officially meet you."

"Mitsy never forgets a face," I told Bobbie. "It's like her superpower."

"That must come in handy." Bobbie perused the selection of cookies, pies, and cakes displayed behind glass.

"Don't let yourself be distracted," I said. "The best thing in this bakery is the cinnamon rolls."

"This is the most cuddles I've gotten lately." Mitsy rubbed her cheek against Kit's fur. "I need to soak it in while I can."

"Is your boyfriend out of town?" I asked.

"We broke up." Mitsy's smile held a touch of melancholy, as if she hadn't decided how she felt about being single.

"You don't sound too upset."

"He wasn't right for me." She paused, then her smile widened. "But now that he's moved out, I can get a dog of my very own. I want a rescue dog just like Kit. Where did you get her?"

Not wanting to spend all morning explaining Kit's complicated backstory, I settled for, "My mother got her for me."

An idea popped into my head. She was single. Kelvin Rutherford was single. Mitsy's cheerful personality might be just the thing to pull the mild-mannered security expert out of his shell.

"One of these evenings when I'm working, you should stop by Sunshine's Tavern. I bartend there when they need me." When she didn't answer right away, I clarified. "It used to be Gypsy's Tavern, but the owner changed the name."

She tilted her head to one side as if thinking it over.

"Sure, why not?" She set Kit down and excused herself to go wash her hands and hopefully brush the dog hair off her apron.

When she returned to her spot behind the counter, I ordered four cinnamon rolls—one for me, one for Bobbie, and two for backup.

As we left the bakery, Bobbie checked the contents of my backpack. She pulled out a small box. "What's this?"

"That's sugar." I showed great restraint by not adding "obviously" or "duh."

"I know it's sugar." She shook the box of sugar packets at me. "How am I supposed to bake with these?"

"Oh, right. Next time, maybe you should be more specific."

"Maybe next time, use your..." She pressed her lips together tightly as if to stop a mean comment from escaping. "Never mind. Let's go back to the General Store. I'm low on eggs, anyway. Although, with the price of eggs these days, I don't know how anyone can afford to bake."

"Scooter doesn't like me taking Kit in there," I said, remembering the way the young clerk had glared at me the last time I tried to sneak her in under my coat. "Why don't I meet you out front in half an hour?"

"I'm just getting a few things," Bobbie said. "It won't take more than five or ten minutes."

"It's like you think I don't know you. You'll run into one of your friends or a neighbor and spend at least twenty minutes gossiping."

"I don't gossip," Bobbie huffed.

"Right. Well, catching up on the local news, then."

Kit tugged on her leash, trying to get to a fire hydrant.

11

"So cliché," I quipped, but let her do her business, then scooped her up and tucked her under my arm.

"Where should we go, Kit?" She gave my cheek a lick, which I took to mean the choice was up to me. "I know just the place."

We turned the corner and headed for Security Plus to see if Kelvin could hook me up with a body cam, or even better, a bulletproof vest.

I pushed the door of the shop open, and Kit and I stepped into the austere, white-walled interior with spotless glass cases, shelves on the wall stacked neatly with surveillance equipment, and an impressive selection of drones.

"Don't pee on anything," I whispered to Kit to be on the safe side.

This was Bobbie's favorite shop for eavesdropping equipment and other gadgets a P.I. in training might need. Kelvin stood by the front window, peering through a pair of binoculars at the bookshop across the street. He flinched and stepped back, a flush spreading on his cheeks.

"Keeping an eye on spiky-haired lady?" I'd spotted her through the window of the bookstore the last time I'd been at Kelvin's shop. He'd claimed the bookshop owner was his arch enemy.

He gave me a shy smile and set the binoculars down. "What can I do for you today? Need to keep tabs on someone? We have a new weather-resistant camera smaller than a matchbox."

"Does anyone use matchboxes anymore?" I wondered aloud.

He shrugged. "Do you think I need to come up with another comparison? A flash drive maybe?"

"What's the story with you and the bookshop owner?" I'd spotted the very blonde and very tanned woman through the curtains on my last visit when Kelvin had dramatically called her his nemesis.

"Nothing. There's no story at all."

I crossed my arms. "I thought you went to school with her."

"Oh right, well, she used to steal my potato chips at lunch. And once she broke some of my crayons."

"That's it?"

He walked behind the counter and busied himself with straightening some of the merchandise.

"Fine." I headed for the door. "Come on, Kit. We're going to the bookstore and have a little visit. Let's see what Kelvin's playmate has to say."

As I turned the door handle, Kelvin called out, "No. Stop."

I turned around and waited.

"I think she's a spy."

Chapter Three

I stared at Kelvin for a long moment. "A spy? You're kidding me, right?"

The firm line of his mouth and tense jaw muscles told me he was going to stick with his ridiculous story.

"What's a spy doing running a bookstore in Arrow Springs?"

"That's a really good question."

"You like dogs, don't you?" I figured I should make sure before I tried to fix him up with Mitsy.

"Sure."

I handed him Kit's leash. "Watch her for me for a couple of minutes, would you?"

Without waiting for him to agree, I pulled the door open and stepped outside, taking a moment to contemplate what Kelvin had said and not said. What did he know that I didn't?

An old man with wisps of gray hair crouched by the

bookshop door fiddling with something—a loose hinge, perhaps, or a squeaky lock. He pushed himself out of his crouch, his knees popping as he stood.

He might have been in a bad mood judging by the glare he shot me. With a grunt, he swung the door open, holding it wide for me.

"Thanks," I said as I stepped inside and assessed the dimly lit space. A few tables stacked with bestselling books took up most of the open area in the front. To the right, a low counter with a vintage cash register held gift cards, bookmarks, and other potential impulse purchases. The rest of the narrow, cramped space held rows of shelves overflowing with books.

As I walked down one of the aisles, something brushed up against my leg, startling me. A fluffy gray cat with a red collar gave me an imperious glance, then disappeared down another aisle. This town was at risk of being taken over by cats if they weren't careful.

The owner, Kelvin's nemesis, wasn't in sight, so I meandered through the aisles. I checked out the cookbooks, wondering if I should buy one for Bobbie, or if she'd see it as a thinly veiled plot to get her to cook more.

Against the wall, a "Local Featured Authors" sign hung above a stack of books. There was only one author featured. Martin Blackwood was the closest thing we had to a local celebrity in Arrow Springs. I picked up a copy of his first memoir. He was a former war correspondent according to his bio and wasn't bad looking, judging by the picture probably taken ten years earlier.

A woman's voice startled me. "Hello."

I swung around reflexively, taking a defensive posture.

It was the spiky-haired lady in a wheelchair. Her blonde hair had an unnatural yellow tone not found in real life, and her arms were as tanned as her face. Considering spring hadn't yet sprung, I figured she must have been a regular at the tanning salon. Between her laugh lines, a few worry lines, and a soft jaw line, I guessed her to be mid to late thirties—although habitual use of tanning beds was aging. Her makeup was impeccable. Not that I'd wear gold glitter eyeshadow this early in the day, but she made it work.

"Hi." I let my arms fall to my side and pretended I hadn't been about to karate chop her. "Nice shop you have. I'm Whitley, but everyone calls me Whit."

"What an interesting name." She offered a small smile. "Much more interesting than mine. I'm Jane Jones."

"At least people get your name right, I bet." Jane Jones sounded like an alias, but that was probably my imagination getting away from me after what Kelvin had said. "I get called all sorts of things, especially Whitney."

She tilted her head to one side. "You're that gymnast, aren't you?"

"Stunt double these days. I'm between gigs at the moment, but after the actor's strike and the writer's strike, it'll take a while for things to get back to normal."

"You're something of a local hero. Herman has a chip on his shoulder when it comes to you, though."

"Herman?"

"My handyman."

"The old guy fixing your door?"

"That's him. He says you lost him some money. He'd

bet that you'd bring back at least one gold medal from the Olympics, but instead..."

Instead, I got kicked off the team when I landed in the hospital from trying to lose too much weight too fast. "That was a long time ago." More than twelve years, but no one in this town would let me forget it.

To change the subject, I asked, "Is that your cat?"

"What cat?"

"The fluffy gray one with the red collar."

Her mouth pursed into a scowl. "Those darned cats keep getting in. I can't figure out how, but when I do..." She left the rest of the threat unsaid and her pleasant smile returned. "Are you looking for anything in particular?"

"Huh?" For a moment, I wasn't sure what she meant, and then I remembered where I was. "Oh right, like a book?"

"We have quite a few."

I chuckled. "No wonder your sign says bookshop. I haven't read much since I got out of school, but I wanted to check the place out. I'm surprised it's still here."

"It stayed closed for nearly five years until I bought it and reopened it last year."

"How interesting," I said, pretending she'd said something interesting. "What did you do before you bought it? Were you in the book business before?"

"No, I did a few different things."

"In Arrow Springs?" I kept my tone casual to keep her from getting suspicious. "I hadn't seen you around before, but I haven't spent much time in town lately."

"I've heard that you can live here for ten or twenty years and still be considered a newcomer."

"You're probably right." Since she'd avoided answering my questions, I tried a different tack. "Do you have any travel books? I was thinking of visiting Russia. Have you been?"

Her smile evaporated. "The travel section is in the back of the shop. You can't miss it. Look around and let me know if I can help you find a particular book."

Jane rolled her wheelchair to the front of the shop, taking her place behind the counter. I wondered why she didn't use an electric wheelchair, and then I wondered why she was in a wheelchair. In the stunt world, we risked permanent injury as a part of our jobs, but Jane didn't seem like someone who would jump off a building. Not that it was any business of mine, but sometimes I couldn't help wondering.

I wandered toward the back of the shop, past seemingly endless rows of shelves. At one back corner, I found the promised travel section and a spiral staircase that led to an upper floor. At the other corner, an unassuming door said, "Used Books." When I opened it, I found a set of stairs going down.

Thinking I might find a bargain cookbook to take home to Bobbie, I crept down the stairs. The musty scent of aged paper hung in the air. The basement was a jungle of shelves packed to the brim with books that had seen better days, with a single fluorescent fixture buzzing overhead.

Books had been stacked haphazardly on bookshelves, shoved in boxes, and piled into towers leaning against the walls. This was not the place to be if we had an earthquake.

As I reached the bottom and turned down an aisle, I heard a rustling noise. I wasn't alone. At the end of the row, I peered through openings in the shelves. On the far side of the small room, a man stood in front of a glass-doored case, flipping through the pages of a book. I didn't feel like chatting with a stranger about literature, so I turned to go back upstairs.

A tickle in my brain told me there was something unusual about the man, so I went back for another look. The pinky on his left hand was a stub, like it had been chopped off at the first knuckle. He might have been born that way, or perhaps it had been a run-in with a power tool. The thought made me cringe.

As I watched, he pulled another book from the case, flipped through it, and put it back. He repeated the process until he opened a small, battered volume. He stopped flipping the pages and a slow smile appeared on his face, then he closed the book and tucked it inside his jacket.

I held my breath as he headed for the stairs. As he passed my aisle, he glanced over and spotted me. His pale blue-gray eyes widened for a split second, then he continued toward the stairs.

He might have planned to pay for the book, but I wanted to make sure. None of the dusty books I'd seen could be worth more than a buck or two, but I wasn't an expert on the subject. Besides, there was the principle of the thing.

When I reached the main floor, I hurried to the front of the shop, arriving just in time to see him rush past the register and out the door.

"He stole a book," I called out to Jane as I followed the stranger. By the time I stepped outside, he'd already reached the next corner. I shouted, "Hey, you!"

He glanced over his shoulder before taking off running. I chased after him, wishing I hadn't eaten so many cinnamon rolls.

Chapter Four

My boots pounded against the pavement and adrenaline surged through my veins as I pursued him down a narrow side street, dodging pedestrians who stopped and stared.

The thief, who had to be in his fifties, was in great shape judging by his speed as he turned the corner. I wasn't about to let a man nearly twice my age outrun me. There was no way he had my endurance, so as long as I kept him in sight, I'd catch him. Then what? I hadn't thought that far ahead.

A familiar barking came from behind me. Kit had sneaked out of Kelvin's shop, dragging her leash on the pavement. She soon caught up with me, and the two of us attracted attention as we ran along the street.

I caught a glimpse of the thief as he ducked down an alley. As I turned the corner, Kit on my heels, he knocked over a stack of wooden pallets in my path. The clatter echoed in the dim alley as I leaped over them. Kit scrambled around the obstacle, determined to keep up.

When the man ducked behind a row of dumpsters, I figured I had him cornered. I approached cautiously, but Kit rushed ahead, snarling and snapping like a fiend.

"Get off me, you mutt," the thief yelled.

Kit yelped just as the man gave the dumpster a shove in my direction. I somersaulted to the side and was back on my feet in a flash in time to see my little dog chasing the man to the other end of the alley.

Rushing after them, I found myself in a crowd of people, some standing, some sitting on the curb, and some in costume. They appeared to be dressed as birds with red plumage wearing blue and white onesies.

I'd forgotten about the parade—the highlight of the Woodpecker Festival. The town had some sort of event practically every weekend. How was I supposed to keep track?

No way was I going to find the thief in this crowd. As I pulled out my phone to locate Kit via the tracker on her collar, I saw a missed call from Kelvin. He'd probably called to tell me he'd let my dog out.

Then I heard her barking not far off. Following the sound, I found her growling at one of the costumed woodpeckers until she spotted a cat chasing another woodpecker and chased after it.

Twenty minutes later, after weaving through the crowd and nearly getting run over by one of the floats, I nabbed Kit. Tucking her under my arm, I headed back.

"You and I are going to have to have a talk," I told her. "This sort of behavior is not acceptable."

Triple Shot

My breathing had finally returned to normal by the time I arrived at the bookshop. Jane Jones looked up, her eyebrows raised slightly in a question.

"I didn't catch him."

Her eyebrows rose higher. "You chased after that guy? For a book?"

"Yeah. I thought it might be a valuable first edition or something, not that I was really thinking. My instincts sort of took over."

"I see." She went back to straightening books on a display table. "I don't have any rare first-edition books here."

"Nothing else of value?" When she answered with a shrug, I added, "At least I got my morning workout out of the way."

Jane wheeled back to her counter, signaling the end of our conversation. I took the hint and left. As I stepped outside, my phone buzzed with a call.

"Hey, Bobbie. What's up?"

"What do you mean, what's up? Where are you?"

"Oops!" I'd completely forgotten I was supposed to meet her at the General Store. "Sorry, be right there."

When I arrived at the General Store, Bobbie scowled at me. "Bernard is waiting for us. And why are you sweaty?"

I pushed the damp strands of hair from my forehead. "Funny story. I wasn't planning to go for a run, but I stopped in at the new bookshop—"

"No wonder you were late," she said, cutting me off. "Next time, you might want to consider someone else other than yourself."

Her comment stung, but I held my tongue for a change. "Wait here with Kit, and I'll run home and get the car. It'll be faster." As an added benefit, the run would let me work off some of the resentment I felt from being unfairly judged.

By the time I returned with my car, I'd nearly forgotten about her barb. On the way to Arrow Investigations, I asked if Bernard had learned anything about who might have shot at Isabella and me. Bobbie told me to be patient.

"I am patient," I said. "I just want to know if they were shooting at me and why. And if they might try again."

The firm occupied an office on the second floor of a dingy strip mall on the edge of town. The best thing about the building was the taco joint on the first floor, which served the best crispy chicken tacos and homemade guacamole in town.

I pulled up in front of the Beauty Shop that advertised twenty-dollar haircuts, and Bobbie was out of the car before I even turned off the engine. I followed her up the stairs and down the hallway to the offices of Bernard Fernsby, Private Investigator. Bobbie pushed open the door and motioned for me to hurry up.

As we entered what might loosely be considered a lobby, a woman emerged from Bernard's inner office.

"Mrs. Needle?" I asked, surprised to run into her again so soon.

"Nettle," she corrected. "I stopped in to ask if Mr. Fernsby could help me solve the mystery of my missing cats. Five of them have disappeared in the last week!"

Triple Shot

"Oh dear." Bobbie tutted sympathetically. "You must be so worried."

Mrs. N. hung her head. "I hate to think the worst, but the stories you hear these days are dreadful."

"No need to think about that. I'm sure we can find out what happened to them and get them back safely."

"Bless you." Mrs. N. squeezed Bobbie's hand and gave me a snide glance as she headed for the door.

"Wait!" I called after her. "I saw a cat today."

"You did?" She brightened up. "Where?"

"At the bookstore."

She sighed. "Lots of bookstores have cats these days. What did it look like?"

I struggled to remember. "It had a red collar."

She sighed again, louder this time. "Then it wasn't one of mine. They all have black collars with tags with my number on them."

"But Jane said—"

Bobbie interrupted me. "I'm sure Mrs. Nettle would like to get on with her day." She ushered the woman to the door, assuring her she'd do her best to help find the missing cats.

Annoyed at being cut off, I followed Bobbie into Bernard's office and took a seat next to her in front of his desk. He waited for us to get settled, his head resting on one or two of his chins.

Bobbie let out a heavy sigh. "We were late because this one," she motioned to me, "decided to go book shopping and forgot all about me."

"I didn't forget," I protested. "I mean, I did forget, but that's because some guy stole a book from the bookstore, and I chased him through town. I lost him when we got to the parade route."

Bobbie's eyes widened. "Why didn't you tell me that sooner?"

"You were too busy scolding me to let me finish what I was saying. Also, Kelvin says Jane Jones is a spy. I mean, it does kinda sound like an alias."

Bobbie's mouth hung slightly open. "What are you going on about? Who's Jane Jones?"

Bernard answered for me. "She owns Birch Street Bookshop."

"Oh, that Jane," Bobbie said. "She's very nice. I had her order a few books for me that she didn't have in stock. I'd much rather give a local business my money than shop online."

I jumped in before Bobbie got started on a rant about the importance of supporting small businesses. "Jane said she opened the bookstore last year. Did she live in town before that?"

"Not as far as I know." She tapped her chin. "I wonder where she's from originally. I didn't detect an accent, did you?" Before I could give my opinion, she turned back to Bernard. "What have you learned about whoever shot at Whitley and her aunt?"

Bernard pursed his lips. "The police are not being cooperative with me on this case. Which means either they've uncovered sensitive information or, more likely, they've got nothing."

"Wallenthorp thinks I made the whole thing up," I said.

"I'm afraid Whitley might be right," Bobbie said.

"Which means they're not going to be any help finding the shooter. Have you been able to learn anything about Isabella Barrera?"

"What about her?" I asked.

"Unless there's someone out to get you," Bernard said, "and you forgot to mention it, your grandmother and I believe it's likely that Ms. Barrera was the intended target."

"Was it a hit man?" I asked. "If that's the case, they have terrible aim."

"Unless the shots were meant to scare her off," Bernard said. "Or as a warning. I haven't been able to turn up any information on your aunt, and without more to go on, there's not much we can do for the moment. I'll keep prodding my contacts on the force."

Bobbie stood and asked Bernard, "What would you like me to work on in the meantime? Search the internet for lost and found reports?"

"Excuse me?" Bernard asked.

"For the missing cats."

Bernard shrugged. "This is the third time she's asked me to find her missing cats. She never wants to pay for my time, mind you," he grumbled. "And besides, they always turn up after a few days."

Bobbie's shoulders slumped. "I suppose I can work on my online private investigation courses. I didn't get much done over the holidays."

"What holidays are you talking about?" I asked. "It's already March."

"So it is, so it is. Time moves faster as you get older."

Chapter Five

I awoke to howling wind, branches scraping on my bedroom window, and a knock on the door. I pulled the comforter over my head to block out the light peeking between the curtains. When the knock was repeated, followed by Bobbie's voice calling my name, I reluctantly poked my head out as the covers wiggled. Kit wasn't happy about being disturbed, either.

"What?" I called back. Being awakened at the crack of dawn always made me cranky.

"I'm heading into town. I want to get to the festival before the lines get too long."

I reached for my phone to check the time. Nine a.m. Not exactly the crack of dawn, after all. "Give me a minute."

Throwing the covers aside, I sat up and rubbed my eyes. Kit's nose poked out, and she peered at me from under the warm comforter. "Sorry, girl. It wasn't my idea."

I shuffled out to the kitchen in my sleep outfit—

leggings and T-shirt. Kit scurried past me, greeting Bobbie by dancing around her as she poured me a cup of coffee. She ran back and forth between us, then to the back door and back again.

"Ugh. Can't I have one cup of coffee before we go out?" I asked the dog.

Kit grabbed the toe of my slipper sock and began to tug.

"Okay, okay." I grabbed my coat from the living room where I'd tossed it over the sofa and told Bobbie I'd be back shortly. Coyotes had been spotted in the area, so no more opening the back door and letting her do her thing on her own. Besides, I didn't trust her. She'd proven to be an expert escape artist, and I didn't want to spend the morning hunting her down.

I stood on the small back deck as Kit took her time intently sniffing bushes, trees, and rocks, some of them two or three times. As I waited, I shoved my hands into my pockets. It never got this cold in Los Angeles, but then, it never got this quiet either. Birds of various sizes and colors entertained me by swooping from tree to tree while a few brave ones hopped on the ground pecking for worms. Eventually, Kit finished her business, and we went back inside.

Bobbie fed Kit while I took a quick shower and dressed, bundling up with plenty of layers. It was supposed to be sunny later, but at that time of the morning, it was barely above freezing. I put her jacket on, but she ran and hid when she saw the booties.

"Don't come crying to me when your feet get cold," I told her. "And I'm not going to carry you either."

As we stepped outside, I blinked against a cold gust of air. "What's with the wind?"

Bobbie scoffed. "You must have heard of the Santa Anas."

I shook my head. "These must be some other winds." The Santa Ana winds were hot, dry, and sometimes extreme, usually happening anytime from September to March. "Otherwise, it would be hot. Or at least warm."

"It'll get warmer by this afternoon."

"Doesn't it usually?" We were halfway down the hill before I took pity on my shivering, whining mutt. "I told you, didn't I? But do you listen to me?"

Bobbie snickered. "You sound just like Angela."

"No, I don't." I did love my mother, but I didn't want to be compared to her, even if it was only the way I scolded my dog.

Most of the snow had melted, leaving brownish icy clumps and mud. Here and there, green shoots poked out from the ground and new leaves appeared on otherwise bare trees.

Kit tugged at her leash, eager to chase a squirrel. "You wouldn't know what to do if you caught it."

As we approached the square, loud music came from the bandstand, where a ragtag mix of musicians belted out fifties and sixties oldies. I recognized members of Kiss My Brass and a fiddler who usually played with the Blarney Band.

The streets around the park had been closed off to traffic. We passed by several shops with their doors wide open and signs out on the sidewalk announcing their Woodpecker Festival special prices.

Bobbie spotted her friends Rosa and Sunshine in front of the hat shop, and we headed their way. Rosa was Bobbie's ride or die, a petite, dark-haired senior citizen who at times seemed to have as much sense as a toddler. Sunshine looked like a troublemaker with her long, wild, silver-streaked hair and red lips, but she was often the voice of reason. I sometimes worked shifts at Sunshine's Tavern with her son Elijah.

Knowing the three women would have plenty of town gossip to share, I handed Kit's leash to Bobbie.

"Would you watch her for a bit?" I asked. When Bobbie hesitated, I gave her my sweetest smile. "Please? I'll be back in a jiffy."

"You'd better," Bobbie said. "She doesn't behave for me the way she does for you."

"If you say so." Kit didn't behave for anyone unless they had a treat for her—or were willing to carry her around like an infant. Lazy mutt.

Kelvin's shop was only a half block away from the square, and I owed him an explanation for running off the previous day, not to mention letting my dog out. As I approached his shop, he threw the door open.

"What happened yesterday?" he asked. "I tried to call you when your dog got out."

"Yeah, I was a little busy at the time. Don't call me for a reference if you apply for a job as a dog sitter," I teased as I walked past him into the shop.

He brushed off my comment. "I saw you take off down the street after some guy. What did he do?"

"He stole a book."

"A book? You chased him for a book?" He squinted through his glasses. "Why?"

That was hard to explain, since I wasn't even sure why. "He ran. So, I ran. At the time, it seemed like the thing to do."

"What kind of book was it?"

"Just an old book. On the small side. It didn't look like anything important, and Jane said they don't have any valuable books in her shop."

"Her name's not Jane."

"It's not?" I asked. "Are you sure?"

"Of course, I'm sure. You don't forget the girl who tormented you for an entire school year. I remember it like it was yesterday. It was third grade. Mrs. Thoman's class at Bailey Elementary in Fairborn, Ohio. Not a day went by without me being poked, prodded, and threatened by her."

I couldn't imagine an eight-year-old's threats could be too terrible, but I wasn't going to tell Kelvin that. "Okay, if she's not Jane, what *is* her name?"

"Marnie."

"Marnie Jones?"

His eyes darted around the room as if the answer was written on one of the walls. He looked back at me and sighed. "I don't remember her last name, but I'm sure it wasn't Jones."

She might have gotten married but knowing her maiden name would have helped.

"Was she in a wheelchair in third grade?"

"No. I have no idea what happened to her after her family moved away." Kelvin returned to the front window and fixed his eyes on the bookshop across the street. "I've been watching all morning. She put the closed sign up a little while ago. It's not even noon and they always stay open until five. I saw some of her book club people go in, but I haven't heard a whisper for nearly half an hour."

"Maybe the book club is a front for a super-secret meeting of the local spy club, and all the spies are sharing all their spy secrets about all the other spies in Arrow Springs. Oh! Maybe the cats that keep sneaking into the shop are spies, too."

"You're making fun of me."

I shrugged. "I'm not saying there aren't spies, but why would a spy move to Arrow Springs? This has got to be the sleepiest town in all of California. Nothing ever happens here."

He raised one eyebrow. "Nothing?"

"Except for a couple of murders, but those were isolated events. Now things are back to their normal boringness. Wait a sec." Something Kelvin had said didn't make sense. "What did you mean when you said you hadn't heard a whisper? How would you hear a whisper from across the street?"

"Oh." He smiled weakly. "I meant that metaphorically. It's been quiet with no one coming or going."

I crossed my arms over my chest. "Kelvin, did you bug the bookshop?" His guilty expression told me all I needed to know. "You did. You devil."

"Okay, yes, I did, but the devices are only on the main floor in the back of the shop. And the basement, but I don't know why I bothered with those since I can't get a signal from them. I should have used a different technology." His shoulders slumped. "The woman you're calling Jane follows me around whenever I go in, so I haven't been able to install them on the second floor."

Recalling the spiral staircase, I wondered how Jane managed to get anywhere but the main floor. "Why would someone who uses a wheelchair open a three-story bookshop with no elevator?"

Kelvin removed his glasses and wiped them with a cloth. "I don't think that's the important question right now."

He could be right, but it did make me wonder if she was able to get around without the wheelchair. Some disabled people only needed mobility aids part time.

"So, what did you hear before it got quiet?" I asked.

"Yelling. It sounded like people fighting, but I couldn't make out the words."

Apparently, I was going to have to pry the information out of him piece by piece. "And then what?"

"The voices faded, and I figured they'd gone to one of the other floors. A few minutes later, someone said, 'At least he won't be a problem anymore.' Then a different voice said, 'No, but now we have a new problem.'"

"What kind of problem?"

"No idea." Kelvin returned to staring out the front window at the bookshop. "That was about ten minutes ago, and since then, it's been completely quiet."

"They might have left out the back way..." I had another idea. "Or they found one of your eavesdropping devices and figured out someone was listening in."

He ignored my comment. "Something fishy is going on and I'm going to find out." He sounded firmly committed to the idea, but he didn't move.

"Now?"

With a stiff nod, he said, "Yes, now."

We stood side by side, staring at the darkened bookshop through the window.

I didn't have all day. "I could go. Just make sure everything's okay over there and report back." I added, "So you don't have to close your store."

His jaw relaxed. "Yes, that would probably be best."

No one answered the door at Birch Street Bookshop. Sidestepping into the shrubbery, I peeked into the dimly lit interior, but there were no signs of life. Back at the door, I knocked again and waited, impatiently shifting my weight from foot to foot. To be thorough, I tried the doorknob. It opened.

Stepping inside, I called out softly. "Hello? Anyone here?" No one answered. "The door was open."

I made my way to the back of the shop. My boots clomped on the hardwood floor.

"Hello?" I didn't want to surprise anyone or be accused of trespassing.

Nothing appeared to be out of place—no overturned bookcases or other signs of a scuffle.

The basement door stood ajar. I told myself now would be a good time to turn around and leave, but I didn't listen to my own good advice. Nothing new about that.

Inhaling sharply, I pulled the door open wider and made my way down the steps. Had the thief returned to steal more books? I didn't for a moment believe the book he'd stolen was worthless, but there was no way to prove it.

Something sketchy was going on in this bookshop, and I didn't like it. An uneasy feeling came over me, but I wasn't ready to leave yet—not without answers. That's when I spotted the shoe.

"Not again," I muttered under my breath. One step closer confirmed the shoe was attached to a leg, which was attached to a man lying unconscious on the floor.

At least I hoped he was unconscious. I stepped closer, hoping to notice signs of life, like his chest moving. My eyes drifted to his hand and his missing pinky finger.

Crouching down beside him, I pressed my fingers to his wrist but couldn't find a pulse. My nose tickled, and I turned away to sneeze before pulling out my phone. The emergency call didn't go through, and a glance at the screen told me why—no signal in the basement.

I registered the sound behind me too late. A sack was thrown over my head and shoulders, plunging me into darkness. As I struggled to break free, a sharp sting pierced my arm.

That really ticked me off, so I drove my elbow into what I hoped was my attacker's stomach. A grunt told me I'd hit the mark, but their hold didn't loosen.

In one swift movement I'd practiced hundreds of times, I stepped back, bending my knees, grabbed my attacker by the neck and flipped them over my shoulder. The thunk told me they fell hard, not to mention the string of obscenities he released.

As I struggled to pull the bag off, the room began to spin.

Chapter Six

A strange dream hovered out of reach—a man with missing fingers had given me a warning. *What was it?* I reached for my pillow and felt hard floor instead.

I forced my eyes open and stared at a ceiling I didn't recognize. Those acoustic tiles with little holes in them reminded me of elementary school when I'd get bored and count them until that task became too tedious. A fluorescent light panel buzzed and cast a cold light on the institutional gray walls. The linoleum floor, flecked with dull blue and red splotches, was thick with yellowed coats of wax.

Where was I? I propped myself on one elbow, my head swimming, and blinked a few times to bring my surroundings into focus. The nearly empty room was barely eight feet square, with two doors and no windows.

I patted my pockets. No phone.

Not trusting myself to stand, I crawled on my hands

and knees to a small stack of boxes in the corner. I opened one. Books. Old books.

I rested against the wall, closed my eyes, and willed my brain to remember. A conversation with Kelvin. The dark and silent bookshop. Climbing the stairs down to the basement.

I pushed up my sleeve and found a small mark where the syringe had pierced my skin. It hadn't been a dream after all. But who had attacked me? And why?

"Questions later, Whit," I mumbled. First, I needed to get out of there. I'd prefer not to leave the way I came in and risk running into whoever'd drugged me. One of the doors looked sturdier than the other and more likely to lead outside.

I crawled over to the door and twisted the knob. "Darn it." The sound of my voice was comforting in the silence, so I kept talking. "Can't kick down a door that opens in. But that door..."

I held onto the wall for support and made my way to the corner of the room, then to the other door. Hoping it led somewhere other than a closet, I reached for the knob. "Surprise, surprise. It's locked too."

This one opened out. Maybe into a closet, but I'd deal with that disappointment when I had to.

On movie sets, I'd kicked down plenty of doors. I had a hunch a real one wouldn't be as easy. At least I'd been taught the right way to do it—a solid kick right next to the handle. Kick the door in the middle, and your foot was likely to go right through it.

So many stunts I'd performed in my career. This was just one more. With no stage lights to blind me and no director yelling, a sliver of doubt crept into my thoughts. Then I remembered what my first stunt coordinator told me.

"Girl, you can kick ass. Never forget it!"

Of course, at the time, I hadn't been pumped full of horse tranquilizers—or whatever they'd used to knock me out.

I took two steps back, sucked in a breath, and landed the kick in just the right spot. The sound echoed in the room, but the door refused to yield.

This time I backed up further to give myself more momentum to make up for my current weakness. I rushed the door and slammed my foot into it.

"Ow." This was a lot easier with fake doors.

A survey of the room convinced me this was my only option. There was no other way out.

"When I get out of here, I'm going to give Bobbie the biggest hug." I could almost hear her nagging me not to forget Kit. "And you too, you little mutt."

What would Bobbie say if she were here right now? She had a seemingly endless supply of aphorisms suitable for all occasions, which most of the time went in one of my ears and out the other.

I heard her voice in my head. "The third time's the charm."

Step, step, kick! With a splintering crack and a groan of hinges, the door gave way. I stepped into ... another room.

My disappointment turned to optimism. This room might not be much bigger than a closet, but it had a window. Sure, it was too high to reach and might be a tight squeeze, especially with all the cinnamon rolls I'd been indulging in lately, but I'd find a way.

Back to the other room, I dragged the boxes one at a time into the second room and stacked them in front of the window in a sort of pyramid. Climbing to the top, I could barely reach the bottom of the window. Even if I were at peak performance, I wouldn't be able to pull myself up without a foothold to steady myself.

The second time I arranged the boxes in an unsteady tower, sacrificing stability for height and carefully climbed to the top. The glass-paned window was the type that swung outward, and I groaned when I saw the latch under multiple layers of paint. It didn't budge, and I didn't have a screwdriver or knife on me. Even a key would work, but I didn't have one of those either.

But I did have a belt. I slipped it out of the loops and used the thingy that goes through the holes as a scraper. The cheap latex paint quickly peeled off, and I turned the latch. I slowly nudged the window open as the boxes under me threatened to topple.

Gripping the window frame, I used all my strength to pull myself up. With my upper body sticking out of the window, I found myself at ground level in the alley behind the bookshop. A quick glance around told me I was alone.

After few shimmies, I squirmed through the window and collapsed onto the ground next to some scraggly shrubs. Exhausted and weak, I felt torn between wanting to rest and an urge to keep moving. What if they came looking for me? I didn't even know who "they" were, but I wasn't about to stick around to find out.

Before I could muster the strength to move, an

umbrella prodded me and a vaguely familiar female voice scolded, "Move along. This is no place for you, whatever you're doing."

Mrs. Nettle, the woman who ran Purrs and Pours, peered at me cautiously, scowling like a disapproving headmistress.

"Hello, Mrs. N." I said, my voice sounding weak to my ears. "It's me, Whitley."

She gasped. "Whitley? What in the world are you doing in the alleyway? You look a fright."

"Thanks." I pulled myself up, leaning on the wall for support. "I'm not feeling that great, to be honest. I was..." Not sure how much to tell her, I finished the sentence with, "attacked."

"Attacked! That's dreadful. Right here?" She straightened up and looked up and down the alley. "I suppose they're gone now. Are you injured? Should I call the paramedics?"

"Yes, but not for me. There's a man in the basement of the bookstore. He's unconscious, or possibly dead."

Her jaw dropped. "Birch Street Bookshop?"

"Is there any other bookstore in town?" I asked. "Would you just make the call?"

"We can call from the café." She turned and headed down the alley, mumbling, "This town used to be safe. First my cats get stolen, and now people are being attacked."

I stayed where I was. "What were you doing out in the alley?" I had good reason to be suspicious, even of a middle-aged cat lady like Mrs. Nettle.

She stopped and turned back. "Well, I didn't know

people were getting attacked out here, did I?" When I didn't answer her rhetorical question, she added, "I was looking for my missing cats, of course."

I was about to say something sarcastic, but that made perfect sense. Besides, my groggy brain was not up for witty retorts just then.

"My café is at the other end of the alley." When I hesitated, she prodded, "Well?"

Without a phone or car keys, I didn't have a lot of alternatives. I shuffled after her, forcing my feet to cooperate. A few doors away, she crossed the alley and entered one of the shops.

"You'll be safe at Purrs and Pours," she said, holding the door for me. "At least until we get to the bottom of what's going on."

Chapter Seven

I followed Mrs. Nettle into the small kitchen of her café, relieved to see it was a cat-free zone.

"Have a seat." She gestured to a couple of folding chairs in the corner. "I'll call Jane and tell her what you told me so she can check the basement."

I sat down and closed my eyes, only to jerk them open when my head bobbed. Sucking in a lungful of air, I blinked hard and willed myself awake.

When she returned and handed me a bottle of water, I gulped it down. "I need to call Bobbie."

Mrs. Nettle pushed a curtain aside and peered into the front room. "We need to be sure the coast is clear. If they find out you're here, they might come looking for you."

"Who is 'they'?"

She turned back to me. "The person who attacked you, of course."

"Why would they come look for me here?" I wondered

if someone had been watching the alley and seen me escape through the window.

She shrugged. "Well, I don't know about these sorts of things, do I?"

I supposed that was a rhetorical question, but either way, she was getting on my nerves. "May I use your phone?"

"Yes, of course. It's on its charger. I don't have a mobile. I like having a landline, even though most people have given them up. I'll be right back."

It took all my strength to get up out of the chair. Bobbie would tell me it was rude to leave without saying goodbye, but I'd come back later and apologize. Or probably not. I tiptoed to the back door, only to find it locked. The deadbolt needed a key from the inside, which was great from a security standpoint, but why had she locked me in?

There might be an innocent reason, but I didn't like being trapped. I pushed through the swinging doors into the front room, startling Mrs. Nettle and a few of the cats. One hissed at me.

"I'm leaving," I announced. "Thanks for the water."

Her face flushed. "I think you should wait for Bobbie. She's on her way."

"Is she?" I asked. "Did you even call her?"

"Well..." she stammered. "I was about to when you burst into the room, upsetting all the cats. They're very sensitive creatures, you know."

"They'll get over it."

She hurried to the door as if to block my way. "I don't think you should leave yet."

"Try and stop me."

The police station was a short walk from the cat café. It would have been faster if I'd run, but I was drained from, well, everything. It's not every day you get drugged and locked in a basement.

When I arrived, I headed straight for the reception window. The desk on the other side of the window sat empty. I buzzed the intercom.

No one appeared, but a voice crackled through the speaker. "Arrow Springs Police Department. How may I assist you?"

"I need to speak with Deputy Wallenthorp. My name is Whitley Leland, and I have a crime to report."

After a long pause, the voice said, "He's not available at the moment."

I clenched my teeth, reminding myself of Bobbie's adage: You catch more flies with honey than vinegar. "May I speak with another officer, please?"

"What is this regarding?"

"I was attacked in the basement of Birch Street Bookshop, not more than..." I looked around the waiting area for a clock and found a man watching me from one of the plastic chairs. In his worn leather jacket and brown baseball cap, he blended into the background, almost as if that was his intention. "Do you have the time?"

He nodded. "Almost two o'clock."

"Thanks." It had been around noon when I'd told Kelvin... Kelvin. Why hadn't he come looking for me?

"Ma'am?" the voice squawked from the speaker.

"I was attacked about two hours ago."

"Who attacked you?"

"That's just it. I don't know."

The intercom fell silent again. I leaned against the wall, tired and frustrated.

The man stood and made his way over to me, his stride unhurried but confident. He was taller than I'd expected, with a lean build and rugged charm. He took off his ball cap and absently ruffled his shaggy brown hair. His amber eyes focused on me, as if daring me to get lost in them. Too bad he wasn't my type... or so I told myself.

Ha! As if mature, good-looking guys with rugged charm weren't *exactly* my type. There was something familiar about his face. I'd seen his picture recently. And then it hit me.

"You're Martin Blackwood."

"Call me Marty." With a hint of a smile, he reached out his hand. I countered by holding out my fist, which he bumped with his. "And you're Whitley Leland. Nice to meet you."

I turned at the sound of the police office door opening. A woman held out a clipboard.

"What's this?" I asked.

"If you'll fill out this complaint, we'll be sure to have someone follow up with you."

I stared at her for several seconds until she became uncomfortable.

"Or you could come back later?" she suggested.

I turned to Marty. "Can I use your phone?"

"Sure."

Bobbie gasped when I told her I'd been attacked and insisted I stay put until she could get a ride to come pick me up.

While I waited, I took a seat next to Marty. "What are you doing hanging around here? Trying to file a police report?"

He chuckled. "Did you tick off Deputy Wallenthorp? Or maybe the entire police force?"

I shrugged. "It's not my fault they don't appreciate me." Mostly, they didn't appreciate me getting involved in their murder investigations. "But you didn't answer my question. Are you a groupie? Do police detectives have groupies?"

"In Afghanistan, I asked all the questions. Almost as many as you do. Now, I'm an aspiring novelist looking for ideas wherever I can find it."

"I saw two of your books at the bookshop. They were bestsellers, right? What exactly are you aspiring to?"

"Those were memoirs of my years as a war correspondent. I should have paced myself better instead of putting all my stories in those two books, but now it's either write a novel or get a real job."

"I'd stick with the novel if I were you." I'd never had anything resembling a nine-to-five job, but I was pretty sure it wouldn't agree with me. "Most jobs are overrated."

"Good advice. Before I sat down to write, I had so many ideas, but staring at the computer, they evaporated into thin air. When I get really desperate, I come here and see who wanders in. So far this morning, it's been a lady asking if there's been any progress on her missing cats—"

"Mrs. Nettle."

He nodded, not asking why I knew her name. "And another citizen reporting a car speeding through downtown. The speed limit is 25 MPH, in case you weren't aware." He smiled, displaying dazzling white teeth. "And now you."

"Ooh, do I win most interesting case of the day?"

"Possibly." His eyes crinkled in a smile. "The day is still young."

Our conversation was interrupted when Bobbie and Rosa burst through the door with cries of, "Oh, thank goodness," and "Are you okay?"

After squeezing me in multiple hugs, Bobbie noticed Marty sitting nearby. "Oh, hello. It's Mr. Blackwell, isn't it?"

"Blackwood." He stood and took her hand gallantly. "But you're not old enough to be Whitley's grandmother."

I rolled my eyes, but Bobbie's face lit up. "I am. Roberta Leland, but you can call me Bobbie. Everyone does."

"And you can call me Marty."

I interrupted the love fest. "Can we go home?"

Bobbie turned and gave me a once-over. She must not have liked what she saw. "I'm taking you straight to the E.R."

"No, you're not." No way was I going to spend the next eight hours in a hospital waiting room. "You either give me a ride home, or I'm walking," I bluffed.

Bobbie pulled me aside, lowering her voice so Marty couldn't overhear. "We need to find out what you were drugged with."

"So call Bernard. I bet he can set up a drive through drug test or something. I don't need to be poked and prodded. I've been through enough today."

She obviously didn't like the idea, but she decided not

to push. "Very well." She called out to Marty, "Nice to meet you."

"My pleasure," he answered gallantly.

I gave him a nod. "See you around."

As I turned to go, he said, under his breath, "You certainly will."

Rosa drove Bobbie and me to a clinic where they drew blood and had me pee in a cup. After that, we swung by the local cell phone provider and got me a new phone, since I was pretty sure my old one was history.

When Rosa pulled up to the house, she turned to Bobbie. "Are you sure you don't need me to stay?" I could tell she didn't want to miss out on anything. A few weeks earlier, she'd told us that things had been boring lately without anyone getting murdered. "Not that I want anyone to die, of course," she quickly added, "but it would be nice if something exciting would happen."

I went inside while the two of them continued their conversation. I'd barely drifted to sleep, curled up on the sofa under an afghan, when someone nudged me. Bobbie suggested I finish my nap in my room.

I yawned. "Nothing like getting attacked, injected with an unknown sedative, and locked in a basement to wear you out."

"I'll wake you when dinner's ready."

Chapter Eight

Sunlight streamed through a gap in the curtains as the remnants of a dream lingered: eight-foot-tall woodpeckers chasing me through the town, throwing books. I rubbed my eyes and shook the images from my consciousness.

Kit greeted me the moment I pushed open the door, then ran past me into my room and reemerged with a sock clenched between her teeth. She whipped it back and forth like a rodent that needed to be subdued, growling like a low powered weed whacker. It was one of her favorite games and I was supposed to try to get it back from her, but I was too groggy. Besides, I never liked those socks.

In the kitchen, I found Bobbie at the table reading the newspaper. Kit bounded into the room, having abandoned the sock, and instead tugged on Bobbie's robe for attention.

She greeted me with a warm smile. "Good morning."

I returned her smile with a scowl. "Why didn't you wake me for dinner?"

"I tried, but you were out cold. I checked to make sure you were breathing and then let you sleep."

I glanced at the clock. "I slept sixteen hours?"

"You must have needed it. Bernard already got the results of the blood tests. It turns out you had propofol in your system. It's a sedative that should only be administered by properly trained medical professionals."

"I'll be sure to check credentials next time someone attacks me with a syringe." I poured myself a cup of coffee and joined her at the kitchen table.

"Would you like to go back to the festival today?" Bobbie asked. "You didn't get to see much yesterday. The costume contest is this afternoon."

"Yeah, it's not really my thing, to be honest." I sensed she was disappointed, so I quickly added, "Unless you want to go."

"Not really. All the different festivals start to blend into one after a few years. It's the same booths, the same food, the same people... Only the decorations are different. At least Founder's Day has a decent costume contest—not just a parade of woodpecker knockoffs."

"I don't remember Founder's Day."

"Probably because it happens in early June before school lets out. It celebrates Franklin Norvelt and his followers who started the community of Arrow Springs back in the 1850s."

"He always sounded like a cult leader to me."

"You're not alone in that opinion." She looked around

the room. "I guess I could give the kitchen a good cleaning." Her eyes drifted to me. "You could help."

At least she didn't add, "for a change." I knew where my strengths lay, and cleaning wasn't it. I was saved from making up new and creative excuses by a knock on the door. When I heard whose voice came from the living room, I might have gloated.

"Hello, Deputy Wallenthorp," I said when the officer entered the kitchen. "What brings you here today?"

He harrumphed. "I understand you visited the station but left without filing a report."

"No one wanted to take my report," I corrected him.

His frown deepened. "I'll be meeting with the staff to review procedures to make sure that doesn't happen in the future. Our department is completely focused on public safety and serving the community, and..." he cleared his throat. "We fell short in that regard."

I had a feeling Wallenthorp's visit was Bernard's doing. Sometimes I wondered if the old P.I. had dirt on everyone in town, or if his years with the police force had earned him the respect of the local officers. I'd lay odds it was the former.

"I understand you wanted to report that someone attacked you. Is that correct?"

As briefly as I could, I gave him a summary of what had happened the previous day when I went into the bookstore's basement and found the man lying on the floor.

"One of my officers stopped by Birch Street Books to talk to the owner." Wallenthorp checked his notes. "Jane Jones said she or her handyman were there the entire day, and nothing unusual happened. She allowed the officer to inspect the basement, and there was no sign of foul play."

"Of course not," I grumbled. "They've had an entire day to clean up and remove any evidence."

That brought a scowl to Wallenthorp's already grumpy face. "She claims someone named Kelvin has been harassing her and suggested this frivolous complaint—her words, not mine—is another one of his attempts to drive her out of town. According to her, he watches her from across the street through binoculars."

"Kelvin had nothing to do with what happened yesterday." I chose not to mention he'd bugged the bookshop. "I'm the one who got attacked."

"Why the delay in making the report?" he asked. "I understand it was two hours later when you visited the station."

I folded my arms over my chest. "There was the little issue of someone sticking a syringe into my arm. I was out cold for probably half an hour or more. And then I had to climb out of a window to escape. Are you going to find out who did that to me, or are you too busy looking for Mrs. Nettle's cats?"

The deputy's jaw clenched. "Are you questioning the department's priorities?"

"Oh, and there might be a dead guy, too. Or did you forget about him?"

Bobbie placed a hand on my shoulder. "Let him do his job, Whit."

"Fine," I huffed. "I'm not stopping him."

Bobbie offered Wallenthorp a seat at the kitchen table. "I'll make a pot of coffee."

If the apocalypse occurred, I was pretty sure Bobbie's first instinct would be to brew a pot. Wallenthorp sat across from me and pursed his lips as if he'd just sucked on a lemon. I sometimes had that effect on people.

"Tell me about the man you found lying in the basement," he said.

"If he wasn't dead at the time, then for sure he is by now, since no one wants to do anything."

"Whit!" Bobbie scolded. "This is no time for attitude. Tell the man what he needs to know."

"Fine," I grumbled.

Wallenthorp gave Bobbie a grateful nod before returning his attention to me. "Can you describe him?"

"You bet. He was in his fifties, I'd guess, probably six feet or close to it. His eyes were grayish blue and really pale. Short dark hair, although I think it might have been dyed." I paused, clutching at fuzzy memories just out of reach. It wasn't an unnatural shade of brown, so what made me think that?

"What else do you remember?"

I closed my eyes and pictured him lying on the floor of the bookstore basement. "He had on a forest green cable-knit sweater, acrylic or maybe a blend, but I'm thinking a hundred percent acrylic." I shuddered. Acrylic had that effect on me. "Oh! And short silver hairs on the sweater. That's why I thought he might have dyed his hair. Maybe he hadn't washed the sweater since his last haircut. That's one thing about acrylic—you can wash it in hot water and dry on high heat and it won't shrink at all." Not that I knew from experience. The one time I'd come home from a mall with an acrylic cardigan, my mother threw it in the trash.

Bobbie set down a cup of coffee and the sugar bowl in front of the deputy.

Wallenthorp stirred two heaping spoons of sugar into his coffee. "That's very specific."

"It's a gift." I got the feeling he didn't agree.

The deputy reviewed his notes as he sipped his coffee. "Why are you so sure the victim was the same man you chased?"

"Oh, that's easy. He was missing most of his pinky."

"Are you sure?"

"Of course, I'm sure. It's not the sort of thing you see every day."

Wallenthorp stood, seemingly done with the interview. "I'll be in touch if I have more questions."

"Or answers?" I suggested. "It would be nice if you'd call us if you find out who attacked me. And why."

"Yes, of course," he said noncommittally.

Bobbie walked him to the door. When she returned to the kitchen, she gave me a stern look. Why was I in trouble?

"What?" I asked.

"I don't want you getting involved. These people are dangerous."

"I guessed that much when I got jabbed with a syringe." I rubbed my arm. "Whoever did it, I don't like the idea of them getting away with it. Oh!" Something had just occurred to me. "What if it was the same person who shot at me?"

"Did you hear the part about not getting involved?"

"I already am involved." I stared into my nearly empty coffee cup, trying to make up my mind if I wanted a refill.

"Bernard and I will investigate, but the man you found in the bookshop basement has nothing to do with you."

I shook my head. "I'm not so sure about that. Is Arrow Drugs open today?"

"Why do you ask?"

"I could use some aspirin." That was true, since I'd had a dull headache since I'd gotten out of bed that morning, but that wasn't why I'd asked about the drug store. "Where's my phone?" Twenty minutes later, I retrieved my phone from between the sofa cushions and looked up the pharmacy hours. They'd be opening soon.

If anyone knew about drugs, it would be a pharmacist.

As long as I had my phone in my hand, I did a search for Isabella Barrera. None of the pictures that popped up resembled her. I tried again with my father's name, Alejandro Barrera, although I had no way of knowing if they had the same last name. Isabella might have gotten married.

Bobbie tapped me on the shoulder. I hid the phone screen from her and looked up to see her holding a glass of water.

"Huh?" I didn't recall mentioning I needed hydration.

She opened her palm. "Aspirin."

"Oh right. Thanks." I took the aspirin and waited for her to leave, but instead she hovered. "What's up?" I asked.

She pressed her lips together for a long moment, then sighed and left the room.

I got back to my research. Isabella had been on the way to the airport to fly to San Diego according to what she'd told me. Had the plane ever taken off? Or was she still in town?

"Hey, Bobbie," I called out from the living room.

She reappeared in the kitchen door, eyebrows raised. "Yes? You summoned me, Princess?"

"I'd rather be queen, to be honest. But that's not important now. I thought I'd stop by to see Kelvin. I never got around to fixing him up with Mitsy. Want a ride into town?"

"You're going to ask him about Jane and the bookshop, aren't you?"

I'd been thinking of asking him about tracking plane flights, but she was right. "That's a good idea, now that you mention it. I'd really like to find out why he didn't come looking for me yesterday."

"I'll come with you."

"Okay, great!" I said with forced enthusiasm. Not only did I want to talk to Kelvin without her, but I didn't want her tagging along to the pharmacy. "Let me put on some shoes and we'll go."

She pointed at the three pairs by the front door. "What's wrong with those?"

"They don't go with my outfit." I headed down the hallway to my room and shut the door before sending a text to Rosa. *Need to ditch Bobbie. Help?* Hopefully, it would appeal to her sense of adventure.

R u sleuthing?

You got it, I answered.

Done.

When I reemerged in the living room, Bobbie scowled at her phone. "Looks like Rosa needs me for something. She's very vague, but you know her. It could be anything from lost car keys to an appendicitis attack."

"Oh, darn." I hoped she didn't notice the lack of sincerity in my voice.

Her eyes narrowed ever so slightly, although that might have been my imagination or a guilty conscience.

Chapter Nine

After dropping Bobbie off at Rosa's, I drove into town, Kit safely strapped into the car seat that Bobbie had purchased for her. When we arrived at Security Plus, the door was locked, so I banged on it. As I peered inside, Kelvin appeared from the back room and held the door open for Kit and me.

I closed the door behind me and let Kit off her leash so she could sniff all the corners. "Still working on your robot army?"

Judging by his humorless, "Ha, ha," he didn't find my joke any funnier than the first time I'd made it. I began to wonder if I was on the right track.

I followed him to the back of the shop, where he preferred to stand behind the counter as if it would protect him from troublemakers like me. "What will you do when you finally achieve world domination?"

He paused to consider my question, then shrugged. "What would you do?"

"I'd start with flying cars. It's a huge disappointment that the greatest advance promised to us by the Jetsons has yet to come to fruition."

He shook his head slowly, as if disappointed by my answer. "Do you ever take anything seriously?"

I grinned. "Occasionally, but I'm best at giving flippant answers, and I believe in leaning into my strengths. But speaking of taking things seriously, why didn't you come look for me yesterday when I didn't come back?"

His forehead crumpled in confusion. "You told me not to."

I folded my arms over my chest. "I'm pretty sure I didn't."

Kelvin pulled out his phone and, after a few swipes of the screen, held it up to see what looked like a text from me.

Everything's cool. See you later.

"Dude," I said, nearly rolling my eyes. "Does that even sound like me?"

He shrugged. "My experience with your texts is limited. It wasn't you?"

"No. I was attacked, injected with a powerful sedative, and locked in the bookstore basement."

His eyes widened. "There was something going on over there. I knew it."

"We need a code word for future texts. Or phone calls."

"How about bunny?" he suggested.

"Bunny?" I waited for an explanation.

"I like bunnies." He paused. "The probability that

either one of us would use the word 'bunny' in a text message is low, don't you think?"

It seemed like as good a word as any. "Bunny it is. And if one of us needs to tell the other that everything is definitely not okay, we'll say, 'Everything's cool.'"

"But that doesn't make sense."

I sighed. "Fine. How about 'coyote.' If you text me, 'I spotted a coyote,' I'll come running."

While Kelvin considered my suggestion, I got distracted by a selection of pistols in a glass case. "Are those real?"

"They're replica firearms. Do you want me to open the case so you can get a closer look?"

"Naw, I already have a prop gun. I accidentally borrowed it from a movie I worked on and forgot to give it back. I keep it in my underwear drawer just in case." Me talking about my underwear seemed to make him uncomfortable, so I changed the subject. "You know about drones and stuff. What do you know about planes? Like specifically, whether a plane would have taken off from the airport in the last two days."

He shrugged. "You could ask the FBO."

"The who?"

"Fixed-base operator."

"Great. Can you call him for me? Or her?"

"The FBO is a company, not a person." He pulled his cell phone out of his pocket and looked up the number.

I dialed it, and after a few rings, a deep voice came on the line.

"Good morning, Big Springs Airport, how can I help you?"

"My name is Whitley Leland, and I had a friend who planned to fly out on Saturday from your airport. She was supposed to call me when she arrived in San Diego, but I haven't been able to get in touch with her. Is it possible for you to tell me if her plane even left?"

"I'd be happy to assist you if I can. Do you have the N-number of the plane?"

N-number? "Um, sorry, no. Her name is Isabella Barrera. Does that help?"

"I'm sorry, but I can't provide personal flight details about a specific individual without their consent."

My hope faded. "Yeah, I get that."

As I was about to give the person a polite thank you and hang up, the voice said, "You say she planned to leave on Saturday?"

"Yes." Hope fluttered in my chest.

"No planes have taken off all weekend. The winds have made taking off and landing unsafe."

"Oh, right. The Santa Anas." For once, I had a reason to be grateful for the dry winds that sucked all the moisture out of the air. I thanked the man and hung up.

"What was that all about?" Kelvin asked. "Who's Isabella Barrera?"

"My aunt. We're not close." That was an understatement. "Thanks for your help, Kelvin. By the way, are you busy tonight? I'm bartending at Sunshine's Tavern. If you stop by, the first round is on me."

"I don't really drink."

"They have good burgers." Maybe he didn't like burgers. "I'll buy you some nachos. Come on, whatcha say?"

He shrugged one shoulder noncommittally. "I'll think about it."

"Aw, c'mon Kelvin. You need to get out more. Get some fresh air. Meet new people."

"I meet people who come in the shop."

"Not like that. I mean, make some new friends." I considered adding, find a girlfriend, but that might scare him off.

His eyes narrowed. "Why is it so important to you if I make new friends?"

"Because I care about you, Kelvin."

"You do?"

Uh oh. Better nip that in the bud before he got the wrong idea. "Yes. You're my friend. And friends care about each other."

He smiled, a rare sight. He really was kinda cute.

On my way home, I sent Mitsy a text. I hoped she liked guys who were nerdy, bashful, and sweet. And possibly building a robot army.

Arrow Drugs, on the same street as the cat café, was the tiniest drugstore I'd ever stepped into. The narrow space smelled faintly of alcohol and menthol mixed in with a hint of lavender from a small display of essential oils.

I made my way down one of the two aisles past neatly stacked shelves stocked with everything from over-the-counter meds to fancy supplements. Labels boasted of miracle cures along with a disclaimer that the product "Is not intended to diagnose, treat, cure, or prevent any disease." Why did people still fall for these snake-oil promises?

Behind the counter, a young man in a lab coat greeted me. "Are you here for a flu shot?"

"In March? Isn't it a little late?" I'd gotten my flu shot last fall at Bobbie's insistence.

"It was worth a shot." He grinned. "Worth a shot? Get it?"

"Ha ha." I wasn't in the mood for cringy puns. "Is Leo Parrigan in?"

He frowned in disappointment. "I'll get him."

The pharmacist appeared, a slender, middle-aged, pasty-complexioned man with glasses perched on his head. He spoke in a pleasant customer service voice. "You were asking for me?"

"I'm Whitley Leland." I watched for his reaction, but all I saw was curiosity. "Is there somewhere we can speak in private?"

He nodded. "In the consultation area." He lifted the hinged counter and stepped out from behind it, gesturing for me to follow him. The "consultation area" was little more than a corner sectioned off with a folding screen. He offered me one of the plastic chairs and we sat facing each other.

"What can you tell me about propa... propafo... Hold on." I retrieved a scrap of paper from my pocket. "Propofol."

He told me what I'd already learned from a quick internet search, that propofol was a prescription sedative and anesthetic to help patients relax or sleep before medical procedures.

"Do you carry it here?"

His mouth opened slightly, and he hesitated before answering. "Why do you ask?"

Following his lead, I answered his question with another question. "Why do you need to know why I'm asking?" I kept talking. "I would think it was an easy question. Do you carry it?"

He pressed his lips together. "No, we don't."

We sat in silence for several moments before I spoke, firmly and with a hint of accusation. "If the police come asking questions, will you give them the same answer?"

He inhaled sharply through his nose. "Please don't go to the police." He swallowed hard. "When we conducted our last inventory, there was a discrepancy. I've been doing my own investigation, but the problem is, we've been shorthanded and missed a couple of inventories, so it's impossible for me to pinpoint when it went missing."

"How many of your employees might have had access to your medications since your previous inventory?"

He shook his head. "At least... ten? We had several pharmacy students working part time and a couple of interns. It's been hard to find permanent, competent help."

Was he telling the truth? No way to tell. "You might want to contact the police and tell them about the missing propofol." I stood to go. "Before I do."

Chapter Ten

The dinner rush had died down when Elijah came over and whispered in my ear—something he found an excuse to do on a regular basis. I didn't mind. After all, the guy was hot, even though he'd made it clear he was only interested in me as a friend, occasional coworker, and someone to practice his flirting on.

"Martin Blackwood just took a seat at the end of the bar. Don't make a big deal, okay?"

"Why would I make a big deal? So, he sold a few books?"

"More like a few million books. He hardly ever comes in here and doesn't like to chitchat, so..."

"No chitchat. Got it."

Elijah gave me one more warning in the form of a pointed glare before delivering a couple of draft beers to one of the tables.

"Hey, Marty," I called out as I headed toward the

novelist, glancing at Elijah to see his horrified expression. "What can I get you?"

"Whit?" Marty gave me a smile, like we were old friends. "You work here?"

"From time to time. Keeps me busy when stunt work is slow. The strikes really put a damper on production."

"No kidding." He gave me a knowing nod. "*The Edge of Shadows* was in pre-production when the writers' strike happened. Now I'm not sure it'll even get filmed." His eyes softened as he studied my face.

"What's wrong?" My hands flew to my mouth. "It's ketchup, isn't it? I didn't have time to eat dinner, so the cook made me a burger."

"No, no ketchup. I was just thinking you'd be perfect in the part of Renne, the street-smart, kick-ass hero. They wanted Zendaya, but with all the delays—"

"Whoa. I'm no actor. I know what I'm good at and that's jumping off buildings and climbing up buildings. Also, jumping from one building to another."

"Just buildings?"

I grinned. "Nah, trees and mountains and stuff, too. Just the other day, I climbed out of a twelve-foot-high window in a locked room."

"Was that for a TV show?"

"That was real life."

He laughed. "You are full of surprises, Whit."

I glanced over at Elijah, who pretended he wasn't listening to every word.

"So, about that drink..." Marty said, reminding me of my current role in society. "How about a whiskey soda?"

"Preference on the whiskey?"

"Surprise me."

He seemed like an Irish whiskey kind of guy, so I poured him a Jameson.

The bar began to fill up as it often did as the evening wore on, so by the time I got back to Marty's end of the bar, he'd finished his drink and was swishing the ice around.

I leaned one elbow on the bar. "Same again?"

"What time does your shift end?" he asked.

"Not for another hour or two."

Elijah interrupted me. "You can head out if you want. I can cover things here." He gave Marty a nod. "Nice to see you, Mr. Blackwood."

I tugged on Elijah's sleeve and whispered, "I can't leave yet. I invited these two friends to come in and I promised to buy them a drink. Do you know Mitsy from the bakery?"

"Of course. We get all our desserts from Sugarbuns."

"I'm trying to fix her up with Kelvin from Security Plus."

"Kelvin? Skinny, pale guy with glasses?" He tilted his head to one side. "You're fixing him up with Mitsy?"

"He's a super nice guy. Anyway…"

"You go, and if they come in, I'll take care of them. It's probably better if you're not here, anyway. You're not exactly subtle."

"What is that supposed to mean?"

"Just go and have fun."

I made my way back down the bar to Marty. "Turns out, my shift is over now."

"Great." He pulled out a few bills and laid them on

the bar. "How about a walk? There's a full moon out. Or maybe you don't like evenings that come with a frost warning."

"I'll grab my jacket."

I headed for the back room, and Elijah followed me. "How do you know Martin Blackwood?"

"We go way back," I teased. "Let's see, it was way back in... Oh, right, I remember now. I met him on Sunday."

"Man, I never would have thought you'd hook up with a rich author."

"What are you talking about? Marty's... well, a little old for me, don't you think?"

Elijah pulled out his phone and did a search. "He's thirty-eight."

"Really? He looks so..."

"Ruggedly handsome?"

"Yeah, I suppose so. But no way he's interested in me. His type dates models or women who look like models. Usually blondes."

I didn't want to keep Marty waiting, so I cut the conversation short. "See you next time."

"I'll want a full report."

I flipped him the bird.

Marty helped me with my parka, a very old-guy thing to do in my opinion. We stepped outside into the crisp, cold air and headed up the street toward the park. I retrieved my knit cap from my pocket and pulled it down over my ears.

Nearly all the snow had melted, leaving muddy patches, which I sidestepped as we crossed the street.

I stopped in front of a huge Ponderosa Pine. "I've always loved this tree. It's so solid, so strong, so resilient…"

"It might have to come down," Marty said as I craned my neck to view the top of the tree.

"What?" I turned to face him, indignant at his suggestion, as if he were the one planning to cut it down. "Why?"

"Pine beetles. The droughts we've had the past several years make the trees susceptible."

"That's sad." I made an about face and headed for Strawberry Lane, which led to the creek. Normally, I wouldn't go that way in the dark, but between Marty and me, I figured we could take anyone who wanted to steal our wallets.

He hurried after me. "I'm sorry, Whit." A few moments later, he said, "I always say the wrong thing."

I stopped and turned to him. "The wrong thing? What was wrong about it? You gave me information that, sure, I didn't want to hear but not telling me that tree is dying wouldn't make it any less true."

"No, but this probably wasn't the right time. I could tell you really liked that tree."

"I did." Why was I upset about a tree? "I think that tree represented something. Something I never had in my life."

"What's that?"

"Stability. Permanence. But now I do have that."

"Ah, you're talking about a person, aren't you?"

I nodded, biting my lip and blinking back the moisture in my eyes. What would he think if I started crying over a tree?

He spoke softly. "I didn't realize you were in a relationship."

For a moment, I had no idea what he was talking about, and then I began laughing.

"What's so funny?"

"I'm talking about Bobbie. My grandmother."

"Oh, Bobbie." His smile returned. "That's nice."

"She's my rock." As much as I wanted to believe that, she wouldn't be around forever. That made me feel vulnerable, a feeling I wasn't used to. "She's no more permanent than that tree. But what she's given me will always be right here." I tapped my chest with my fist. "And one more thing. I don't like people who always say the right thing. I don't trust them."

With the moon lighting our path, we walked in silence, heading toward the sounds of the gurgling stream.

"Do you want me to show you where Kit found a dead body?"

"Wait." Marty stopped in his tracks. "Who's Kit?"

"I forgot you haven't met Kit yet. She's my dog. I figured since you were desperate for material for your book, it might help your writer's block."

"Your dog found a body." He shook his head in disbelief.

"Yep, she led me right to it."

"Tell me more." Before I could say anything, he added, "Unless you'd rather not talk about it."

"Are you kidding? It was some of my finest investigative work. Although, my skills could be summarized by asking too many questions until the murderer decides you might be onto them and need to be eliminated."

"I hope you've learned your lesson."

"I hope so too, but probably not. The strangest case is the one we're working on now, except we're not really working on it at all because Bobbie says it's too dangerous."

"She's right. This is about you being attacked at the bookshop, isn't it?"

My danger meter went off. "Who told you about that?"

"I was at the police station when you tried to file a report, remember?"

"Oh, right." I took a few slow breaths. "I haven't been the best judge of character in the past. Especially with men. It nearly got me killed once or twice. What I'm trying to say is, it might take me some time before I can fully trust you."

Marty gave my hand a squeeze. "I'm in no rush." After a meaningful pause, he grinned. "Now why don't you show me where your dog found that body?"

I'd set my alarm to go for an early run. Good thing, too, because all heck broke loose by the time I got back.

Bobbie spoke into the phone as she paced from one end of the kitchen to the other. "I told you, Rosa, I don't know who he is." She paused. "I've told you everything I've learned so far." Another pause. "You're perfectly safe, but if you're that worried, lock your doors and pull your drapes. I'll call you when I have more details."

She ended the call and gave me an exasperated look.

"A body washed ashore at the lake." Her phone began ringing, but she ignored it.

"Whose body?"

"A man. That's all I've been able to find out."

Her phone began to ring again as I filled my coffee cup.

"Whenever anything happens in town, everyone always calls me for the news."

Gossip, she meant, of course, but I didn't correct her.

"You can silence the ringer if you want."

"And miss an important call?" The phone rang again, and after glancing at the screen, she answered it. "What have you got?"

A man's voice answered. Bernard, I guessed, though I couldn't make out his words.

Bobbie sat down at the kitchen table, her demeanor shifting from impatience to wonder. "Is that so?"

"What is it?" I asked.

She waved me off. After a few more cryptic questions on her part and answers I couldn't hear, she hung up. "You'll never guess who the dead man is."

"You underestimate me."

"Is that so?"

"It's the thief with the missing pinky."

Chapter Eleven

Bobbie, Kit, and I arrived at Arrow Investigations, where Bernard confirmed that the man whose body had been found had a missing finger. The police had identified him as Daniel Holland, a thief who specialized in high-ticket items such as jewels, valuable paintings, and historical artifacts.

"Was there water in his lungs?" Bobbie asked. "If not, that would mean he was dead before he ended up in the lake."

"The cause of death is listed as blunt force trauma, not drowning." Bernard flipped through his notes. "No other details, at least none that the police would share with me."

"Murder, then."

"Most likely."

I piped up. "When did he die?"

"Let's see... The Medical Examiner's preliminary estimate is Sunday between approximately ten a.m. and four p.m. I imagine not knowing when he ended up in the lake makes time of death harder to estimate."

I didn't need an estimate. "I'd say he died right around noon."

Bernard nodded. "About the time you found him lying in the bookstore basement? That makes sense."

Bobbie tutted her disapproval. "Maybe you'll do a little less poking around in the future. You're my only granddaughter, and I've gotten rather attached to you. You could have been killed."

That was sweet and all, but I was focused on the thief. "If he likes to steal expensive stuff, why did he steal a book?" It didn't make sense.

"Good question," Bernard said. "Either that book was worth a lot of money, meaning thousands of dollars, or Holland thought it was. He didn't dabble in petty theft."

"Why would anyone keep a valuable book in a cabinet in the basement? Wouldn't you keep it locked away somewhere safe?"

"What if she didn't know what it was worth?" Bobbie asked.

"Oh!" I had an idea. "What if the book was meant to lure Daniel out of hiding? She could catch him trying to steal it. Brilliant, right?"

Their blank expressions told me my idea didn't impress them.

"How would they manage for Daniel to get ahold of that information?" Bobbie asked.

"Hmm..." I hadn't thought that through completely. "Someone Jane knows could befriend him and tell him they'd learned that she had a very valuable book."

Bernard shook his head. "I doubt that Daniel would be fooled that easily."

I wasn't giving up yet. The stolen book had something to do with why Daniel was murdered and I was attacked. I was sure of it. How had he found out that it was valuable?

"Let me know when you learn more." Bobbie stood and shook Bernard's hand, then turned to me. "Whit?"

"Huh?" I'd only been half listening.

"Let's go home and—"

"Cats!"

"Excuse me?" Bobbie asked.

"I bet Daniel used cats to eavesdrop on Jane. When I was there, she said they kept getting in. The one I saw had a red collar, and I bet you anything that there was a bug on that collar." I waited for one of them to laugh at my theory.

"It's not the wackiest idea you've ever come up with, Whitley," Bernard said, exchanging a glance with Bobbie.

I jumped up from my seat. "It's a long shot, but he might have bought the bugs in town." And if he did, I knew where he got them.

A quick visit to Security Plus confirmed that someone had recently purchased two dozen long-range miniature eavesdropping devices.

While Kit squirmed to get down from my arms, Kelvin handed one of the bugs to Bobbie, who turned it over in her hand.

"That's definitely small enough to go on a cat's collar," she said.

"Are you saying someone used cats to eavesdrop?" Kelvin asked. "That's sort of brilliant. Although, when the CIA tried it back in the 1960s, it didn't go so well. After investing about twenty million, they realized cats can't really be trained."

"They had twenty million cats?" I asked, stunned.

Bobbie snorted a laugh. "I'm pretty sure he meant dollars."

"That makes more sense. I mean, where would you keep them all? Imagine cleaning all the litter boxes."

Bobbie interrupted my musings. "Focus, Whit."

"Right." For a moment, I'd forgotten why we were there. "Who bought the bugs?"

He didn't answer right away. Instead, he disappeared into the back room and returned with his laptop.

While he clickety-clacked on the keyboard, I paced the shop impatiently. Bobbie calmly perused the items in the long glass case.

"Check out the tasers, Whit." She waved me over. "Do you think I should get one?"

"Oh, sure, why not?" I figured I might as well humor her. "You never know when you're going to need to taser someone. Are they legal here in California?"

"They are," Kelvin said, not looking up from his computer. "Though you can't carry one in certain areas, like schools."

"I bet some of the teachers are disappointed about that," I said. "Pepper spray might be more practical."

Bobbie's eyebrows shot up. "For teachers?"

I snickered. "I meant for you."

Kelvin's blank expression made me question if he had a sense of humor at all. "I've found the guy's name."

"Great." I walked over to him and waited expectantly, but apparently, he needed prompting. "What is it?"

"I can't share customer data with you. A lot of my customers expect discretion. After all—"

I interrupted him before he chose to recite his privacy policy. "Can you at least tell me if his name is David Holland?"

"Daniel," Bobbie corrected.

"Right. Daniel Holland. Can you tell us that much?" I added, "Pretty please," for good measure.

"He's the man whose body washed up on the lake bank this morning," Bobbie said matter-of-factly, as if that sort of thing happened every day. "Any information you can provide might help us solve his murder."

Kelvin hesitated. "I suppose I can do that much. The buyer's name isn't Daniel Holland."

I turned to Bobbie. "That doesn't make sense." My mind churned with possibilities. Could all my theories have been wrong? "On the other hand, if it was Daniel who bought the bugs, he would have used an alias." I grinned, happy to be back on the right track. "Can you describe him? Like, did he have all his fingers?"

Kelvin gave me a sideways glance at that question. "It was an online order. I never saw the guy."

"Dammit."

"Language, Whit," Bobbie scolded.

"I said dammit without the 'n'—as in, 'The river's about to overflow. Well, dam it!'"

Bobbie shook her head, no doubt astounded by my quick logic. "Can you give us the person's address?"

"Good question," I said, although I doubted that Kelvin was going to share that info. "We can pop in for a visit."

Kelvin glanced again at his screen. "It was a USPS mailbox."

Bobbie sighed. "I suppose that's a dead end. The post office will be even less forthcoming than you have been." Ever the diplomat, she quickly added, "Not that I don't appreciate your help."

I wasn't done trying. "What city is the P.O. Box?"

Kelvin didn't have to look it up. "Arrow Springs."

"Okay, it's not exactly proof." In fact, it was far from proof—but I wasn't about to let that stop me. "The buyer must have been Daniel. It's too much of a coincidence otherwise. He put the tiny bugs he ordered from you on the cats' collars and then let them into the bookshop."

Kelvin tilted his head to one side before asking, "Where did he get the cats?"

"That's the easy part," I said.

"Of course." Bobbie tapped the side of her forehead. "He stole them from Mrs. Nettle."

The walk to Purrs and Pours was only a few blocks, but Bobbie began to lag behind.

"Why do you insist on walking like you're in a hurry?" she asked. "We've got plenty of time."

Reluctantly, I slowed my pace. "How well do you know Mrs. Nettle?"

"Let me see." Bobbie took the question as an excuse to stop walking. "She's been in town since before I moved up here full time. The cat café is a relatively new venture, though. I suspect she needed a place to keep all her cats. She's too soft-hearted—can't say no anytime someone finds a litter of kittens no one wants or when someone passes away and the family doesn't want to keep the cats."

"After I was drugged and escaped, she sort of appeared. Quite a coincidence, don't you think?"

"A lucky coincidence, I'd say."

When we reached the café, Bobbie groaned. "It's closed. Now we have to walk all the way back to the car."

"Since when are you such a lazy bones?" I asked, using one of the names she used to tease me with when I was a kid. "This isn't like you."

She sighed. "It happens every winter. After being cooped up indoors, it takes me a while to get my stamina back."

"Next winter, we're not going to let that happen, even if I have to drag you to the gym three times a week."

"Next winter?" she asked. "You're planning to stay in town a while longer?"

"I can at least visit more often." Pressing my face against the window, I peered inside and tapped on the glass. "Where do the cats go when the café is closed?" Without warning, a cat lunged at the window. I let out a squeal as I jerked back and tripped, falling on my backside.

Bobbie rushed to my side. "Are you okay?"

After making sure nothing was broken, I stood. "Nothing damaged but my ego."

Chapter Twelve

That night, I went to bed planning to sleep late. Instead, the buzz of my phone woke me shortly after sunrise. I rolled over to grab it, waking up Kit, who peeked out from under the warm comforter.

The text was from Marty. *Plans for this morning?*

Seeing his name on my screen brought a smile to my face and a warm glow inside, which triggered warning bells in my head. What did people always say? Not to see too much of someone at first? I replied to his message. *Sorry. Busy with detective stuff.*

Too bad. Was gonna buy you a cat-puccino.

Cat-puccinos meant Purrs and Pours, and I'd been wanting to question Mrs. Nettle ever since our weird encounter after I escaped from the bookstore basement. I had a feeling she knew more than she was letting on.

What a coincidence, I typed. *Have q's for Mrs. N. Meet you in 20.*

Kit ran to the door, then back to me, tail wagging, while I slipped into the black jeans and T-shirt I'd worn the day before. She grabbed one of my socks before I got to it and shook it forcefully.

"I'm pretty sure that sock is dead by now." I reached out, and she dropped it at my feet. I scratched her behind one ear. "Good girl."

Bobbie sat at the kitchen table with her coffee and the newspaper. "Good morning, you two rascals. Did you sleep well?"

"I slept great. Pretty sure Kit did too, but you'd have to ask her yourself." Grabbing my parka from the coat closet, I told her I was running some errands.

"Aren't you forgetting something?" When the only answer she got from me was a confused expression, she reminded me that Kit needed a potty break.

Kit slipped between my legs the moment I opened the back door. The dry wind kicked up dead leaves, and tree branches swayed gently, their nearly barren twigs just beginning to bud. It was too warm for my parka, which gave me hope that spring weather had finally arrived. Kit sniffed all the bushes, looking for the perfect one to pee on, avoiding patches of snow that lingered in shady corners.

While Kit did her business, I planned what to ask the cat lady. I'd learned it was best to start out non-confrontationally and win people over before asking the tough questions, but my impatience often got the better of me.

"What's your deal, Mrs. Nora Nettle?" I said out loud, and another question came to mind. "C'mon Kit. Time for your breakfast."

At the sound of the last word, her ears perked up, and she hurried to the door.

Returning to the kitchen, I asked Bobbie, "Is there a Mister Nettle?"

She looked up from her newspaper. "Hmmm. I suppose there must be, or at least there once was. I've never met him. What made you think of Mrs. Nettle?"

"No reason." I didn't tell her my plans in order to save myself from another lecture about not getting involved.

"If you have time, there's oatmeal on the stove. It should still be warm."

"Thanks, but—" My phone buzzed, and I pulled it from my pocket. Another text from Marty.

P&P not open until 9. See you then.

"Oatmeal sounds great."

Bobbie had set out the butter and brown sugar. Oatmeal was supposed to be healthy, but not when I got done doctoring it.

"Spring is really here," I informed her in between bites.

"There'll be one more frost before we're done with winter. I can smell it."

"You can smell the future?" I put my bowl in the dishwasher. "That's a cool trick. I can't wait to see how you use it to defeat the bad guys."

Bobbie gave me a long, sideways look before returning to her paper.

The parka went back into the coat closet, hopefully until next winter. I grabbed a zippered sweatshirt and stuck my head in the kitchen. "See you in a bit."

Bobbie looked up from the crossword puzzle. "Why don't you take Kit with you?"

Thinking fast, I said, "I would, but I'm going to stop in at the general store, and you know how strict they are about dogs."

She set the paper down. "Would you pick up a half gallon of milk while you're there?"

I forced a smile. "Of course."

"Oh, and we're low on mayonnaise." She got up to check the refrigerator. While she was there, she took inventory while I tapped my foot in a not-so-subtle sign for her to hurry up.

Several minutes later, I tucked Bobbie's list in my pocket and headed into town. Funny how the signs of spring were everywhere now that I was aware of them. Green shoots poked out between cracks in the sidewalk, and the trees and bushes were covered in buds.

Several curious cats greeted me as I stepped inside the cat café, sniffing my shoes and pant legs. Mrs. Nettle spotted me from across the room and hurried over. The hot-pink sweatshirt she'd chosen for the day featured an illustration of an evil-looking white cat and the words, *Fluff Around and Find Out.*

"Whitley. What are you..." She paused as if rethinking her question. She forced a smile and started over. "What a nice surprise to see you. Can I get you something to drink?"

"Not right now." A cat rubbed against my leg, leaving orange fur on my black jeans. "I'm waiting for a friend."

Her smile widened. "Oh good. Are they interested in adopting?"

"Adopting?" It took me a moment to realize she meant adopting a cat. "I'm not sure. He invited me to meet him here."

One of the sofas had a view of the door and the sidewalk outside, so I made myself comfortable while waiting for Marty. Without Kit to keep them at bay, the cats surrounded me, sniffing like I was a newly opened can of salmon. Some rubbed against my legs while others jumped up on the sofa next to me. A sleek black cat climbed on the back of the sofa and began kneading my shoulder. It felt kind of good, until he got reckless with his claws.

"Ouch! Stop that." I gently pushed the cat away, but it must have thought I was playing with it, because it pounced at me. I pushed it away again, and it pounced again, giving my ear a nip. "Ow!"

"That's Midnight," Mrs. Nettle said. "She's still a kitten, really. Very playful. Midnight's not a very original name for a black cat, but her new owner will probably want to give her another name, so I don't spend too much time coming up with a perfect name for them anymore."

"Who's that?" I pointed at the furless creature staring at me from across the room. It looked more like an alien than a cat, with a bulbous head and wrinkled skin. It stared at me with bulging eyes, blinking slowly, as if it were plotting something devious. "She's watching me."

Mrs. Nettle chuckled. "Lucifer is a sweet cat. So misunderstood. I don't understand why she has such a bad reputation."

I was about to suggest changing the cat's name, but I doubted that would help. The cat licked its paw, not taking her eyes off me.

With a shiver, I turned back to Mrs. Nettle. "By the way, is there a Mr. Nettle?"

She stiffened. "Why do you ask?"

"No reason. Is he dead?" I watched her mouth drop open. It probably would have been best to wait for Marty before I asked any more questions, but I couldn't shut up. "You're probably divorced. Plenty of people get divorced these days," I rambled. "There's nothing to be ashamed of. Not that it's any of my business."

A wave of relief washed over me when I spotted Marty pushing open the door.

He gave me a little wave. "Hello, Whit. Hello, Nora."

Mrs. Nettle brushed invisible crumbs off her sweatshirt. "Nice to see you again, Mr. Blackwood."

"Marty, please."

Her cheeks reddened. "Yes, yes, of course. What can I get you?"

He raised his eyebrows in my direction, and I nodded. Whatever he ordered, I wasn't going to drink it. I liked my coffee without cat hair.

"Two cat-puccinos, please."

He sat down across from me and waited for Mrs. Nettle to be out of earshot. "Have you started your interrogation yet?"

"That's an aggressive word," I said. "I prefer 'inquiries.' And I haven't asked her much of anything. Well... except I did ask if Mr. Nettle was dead."

He did his best to hold back a snicker. "Is he?"

I shrugged and leaned back on the sofa. "I never found out. She got flustered, then I got flustered and started rambling. Good thing you showed up when you did."

He reached down to pet a gray shorthair cat. "Do you think Mrs. Nettle's missing cats are connected somehow to the bookshop?"

"Possibly..." How much should I tell him? "Do you?"

A Siamese rubbed against his legs. "If Nora were a character in my novel, she'd be the head of some clandestine organization, and the missing cats would be misdirection—a sort of red herring."

"Are you planning to put this into a book?" I didn't like the idea of being used for research.

He lowered his voice. "I kind of wish Nora was at the center of a secret plot that I could expose with a featured article in the *New York Times*. Real life is hardly ever that interesting."

His comment about a secret plot reminded me of joking with Kelvin about the secret spies and their secret meetings. "My real life has been pretty interesting lately, and not in an entirely good way."

I sneezed as Nora arrived with our drinks. Midnight leaped from the back of the sofa to the coffee table and stuck her nose into my cup.

"Stop that!" Mrs. Nora picked up the cat, which now had a foamy milk mustache. She set Midnight on the floor and gave it a scolding. "The people drinks aren't for you. We've had this discussion several times before, and I'm starting to think you aren't listening to me. If you don't learn to behave, it's not very likely you're going to find your forever home."

Marty gave Nora a warm smile. "Can you spare a minute or two and join us?"

"Me?" She flushed and fluttered as Marty pulled over another chair.

Marty's expression turned as serious as someone attending a funeral. "When I was at the police station, I overheard you mention some of your cats had gone missing, and I'm sure you must be worried. Have you heard anything?"

Nora gave him a sad smile. "It's so kind of you to ask."

Wow. I could learn a thing or two from this guy about buttering people up. I'd also need to watch out for him trying the same tactics on me.

"Most of them came back, thank goodness, but Smoky, Mittens, and Puff-puff are still missing." She hung her head. "I'm worried sick about them." She wiped away a tear from the corner of her eye as she stroked a long-haired orange cat. With each stroke, tufts of fur floated into the air, swirling around the cat like a fuzzy cloud.

As I sneezed again, a vision popped into my head of gray hairs on an acrylic sweater.

"Are any of the missing cats silver-gray?" I asked.

Mrs. Nettle brightened. "Puff-puff is a beautiful Persian mix. The sweetest little fluff ball you've ever seen." She closed her eyes as if lost in a memory. "She lounged around like a princess, especially if she found a patch of sun coming through the windows. She really was a princess in a previous life, reincarnated from—"

"I need to go." I stood and told Marty I'd wait outside, then maneuvered around the cats and slipped out the door, where I paced the sidewalk until he appeared moments later.

"Why'd you rush off in such a hurry? I made our excuses and—"

"Yeah, I didn't want to get her hopes up, but I'm pretty sure I know where the missing cats are. Or possibly were. Also—" I sneezed again. "I think I might be allergic to cats."

Chapter Thirteen

When I said I knew where the missing cats were, I didn't exactly have a street address, but I hoped that wouldn't be too hard to find.

I called Bernard. "Do we know where Daniel Holland lived?" He didn't but promised to call me back if he managed to get the information.

After I hung up, Marty asked, "You think the dead man stole Nora's cats?"

"Yeah, but before he died." Obviously.

"Why would he... why would anyone steal somebody's cats? People give away kittens by the boxful in front of the grocery store."

"He needed full-grown cats. Tame ones." I explained about the cat I'd seen at the bookshop. "Somehow, he suspected that there was something worth stealing at the bookshop, something very valuable, and he used the cats to find out exactly what it was and where to find it."

He gave me a blank stare. "But... cats?"

"My theory is he put tiny devices on their collars, then snuck the cats into the bookshop and listened in on Jane until she threw them out."

"Fascinating."

I couldn't tell if he meant it or if he was humoring me. I'd give him the benefit of the doubt for now. My phone buzzed with a text from Bernard.

"I got the address." I put it into my phone and pointed north. "About half a mile that way. We can walk, if that's okay with you."

At the outskirts of the business district, we turned down a residential street lined with rustic cabins and a-frame homes. As I followed the directions from my phone, I began to think we were going in circles.

"What's with the streets in this town?" I asked as we walked toward a stone cottage. "Didn't we already pass that house?"

"Our topography doesn't lend itself to a grid of streets all at right angles to each other. Let me see if I can figure it out." Marty reached for my phone. "I've walked up and down nearly every street within a mile of downtown."

Marty finally got us to the right place. The house stood hidden behind a thicket of fir trees. It was one of those story-and-a-half designs where, instead of an attic, the upper floor was used as a second bedroom or studio. The siding had been stained dark brown with white trim that was peeling in places.

"It's not much to look at, is it?" I commented as we climbed the steps to the small front porch and approached the door. "I don't see a doorbell. Might as well knock and see if anyone's here."

"Who are you expecting to answer?" he asked. "Mrs. Nettle's cats?"

"Very funny. The landlord might be here getting the place ready for a new tenant." I knocked three times, hard. "Or the police. I don't want to walk on in and find Deputy Wallenthorp waiting for us."

"Good point. I'm sure they've searched the house and collected any evidence. They would have done that as soon as they identified the body."

"If you say so." Sash windows flanked the front door, and I peered through each in turn. "If the police found cats, you'd think they would tell Mrs. Nettle."

"She's been to the station enough times. They'd have to figure they were likely to be hers."

"She even wanted to hire Bernard to find them." I tapped on the glass. "Here, kitty, kitty."

No cats came running, which didn't surprise me. I tried the door, which was locked, then the windows. Marty had already made his way back down the front steps around the back. I joined him at the back door, which was also locked.

"Now what?" he asked.

First, I checked if the nearby houses had a view of what I was about to do. Curious neighbors often called the police, and I didn't want them showing up just yet. One neighbor might have a view of us from their upper floor, but I was willing to chance it. I stood as far back as the sloped lot allowed and assessed my options.

"Why not pick the lock on one of the doors?" Marty suggested.

I turned to him hopefully. "You can pick locks?"

"I figured you could."

"I've never needed to since everyone in this town seems to..." Of course, a hidden key. Why didn't I think of that sooner? "Help me search for a spare key. Leave no stone unturned. Literally."

After several minutes, all we'd unearthed were a few insects who didn't seem happy about being disturbed. We gave up, and Marty followed me back to the rear of the house.

"I'm going to hope that window isn't locked." I pointed to a sliding aluminum window on the upper half-story. "Most people wouldn't see any need to lock it."

"For good reason," Marty said. "There's no way anyone could get up there."

I grinned. "Watch me."

Chapter Fourteen

Marty gave me a doubtful look. "How are you getting up there without a ladder?"

I chuckled. "I forgot you've never seen me in action."

Eyeing the back of the house, I planned my ascent. I could grab onto the roof overhang below the window and shimmy the rest of the way, but that was two feet too high for me to reach. I'd climb up one of the posts, but why make it harder than it needed to be?

Marty followed my gaze to the upper floor. "What if someone shows up while you're breaking and entering?"

"I'll just tell them I'm worried about the cats and want to make sure they're not trapped with no food or water."

"Right." He didn't seem convinced. "You think that'll work?"

"We'll find out when the time comes. How about a boost?"

Marty raised his eyebrows. "A what?"

I put my hands on my hips. "Don't tell me you've never given someone a boost before."

"Not since grade school."

He crouched down and locked his fingers together. With one hand on his shoulder, I stepped up into his cupped hands and pushed myself up, holding onto the post for balance.

The overhang was a few inches out of my reach. "Higher."

Marty grunted as he lifted me, and I grabbed the edge of the roof overhang, my fingers curling tightly around the rough wood. It felt solid under my grip, and I hoped the years hadn't turned it brittle. I braced my feet against the side of the house for leverage and pulled upward with all the strength I had, just like the jump to front support I'd learned to do in gymnastics—only without the jump. I almost pointed my toes out of habit.

Lying flat against the asphalt shingles, I pulled my knees up to my chest one at a time and hooked my feet onto the edge. I grabbed onto any handhold available and inched toward the window with slow, deliberate movements.

The narrow window slid open easily, and I gave Marty a thumbs up. It was a tight squeeze and took some twisting to get inside. I landed on my side with all the grace of a walrus. The upper floor was small and only partially finished, with a battered-looking metal desk in one corner. After a few moments to catch my breath, I took the stairs to the main floor and unlocked the back door for Marty.

"There's the proof." I pointed at a food and water dish on the floor, then opened the cupboards, looking for cat food. Meanwhile, Marty explored the rest of the house.

After I'd found a stash of cat food and several red collars, but no eavesdropping devices, I checked out the sparsely furnished living room—a sofa that had seen a decade or two of wear, a wood veneer coffee table, its surface marred by scratches and water rings, and a floor lamp that leaned to one side.

"Hello?" The voice came from the kitchen. "Is someone here?"

"Oh, crap." I forced a friendly smile and headed for the back door to find out who'd wandered in.

The woman, at least sixty years old and wearing a ruffled apron over a blouse and jeans, started when she saw me. "What are you doing here?"

"I was worried about the cats."

"Oh," her shoulders relaxed, and she let out the breath she'd been holding. "Me too. I warned him that I'd seen a coyote, but I'm not sure he listened. When the police came, they let me call an animal rescue to come get the cats. I didn't want them to end up at the pound. Did you know him?"

At first, I wasn't sure whether she meant the police or the coyote. I almost said, "the dead guy?" but caught myself. "I only knew Daniel in passing."

In hushed tones, she said, "They say he was a thief!"

"That's what I heard, too." I did my best to sound appropriately shocked and shook my head disapprovingly. "You never can tell about people these days, can you?"

Marty came from the other room.

"Oh!" the woman squeaked before a hint of a smile appeared on her face. "Are you...Martin Blackwood?"

Marty extended a hand. "You must be one of Daniel's neighbors. We were, um, checking on the cats."

"Yes, Marty," I said. "I just explained that to the nice lady."

"It's so thoughtful of you to be worried about them. The rescue told me they'll do their best to make sure they find good homes."

"What a relief," Marty said, looking appropriately concerned.

They continued commiserating about the poor, unfortunate cats while I waited for a chance to get rid of the woman and finish my search.

"I don't suppose..." she began, then hesitated. "Your book is this month's selection for our reading group. I told the other ladies we should invite you to one of our meetings, but they said you'd never come, that you're too famous and a recluse." Her hand flew to her mouth. "Oh, I'm sorry. Sometimes when I get excited, I can't stop talking."

Marty turned on the charm like he was flipping a switch. "They're right, really. I am a bit of a recluse. I prefer to keep to myself, to be honest."

"If you wouldn't mind terribly, would you sign my book?" She pressed her lips together as she waited for his answer. "I'm right next door."

"Yes, of course. Lead the way."

As they left out the back door, I heard her say, "when they hear that I had you over to the house for tea..."

Sometimes, I found it annoying to be overlooked, but other times, it worked to my advantage. I resumed my search in the bedroom, where two cheap, wood-grained nightstands flanked a queen-sized bed, a little saggy in the middle. The drawers of both nightstands were empty. The same was true for the closet, which had been emptied of its contents—but by whom?

In the bathroom, a thin bar of soap sat next to the sink, and the medicine cabinet held a stick of deodorant, tweezers, and a small bottle of antacids.

I returned to the bedroom. It was a cliché to hide things under your mattress, but I'd looked everywhere else, so I lifted the mattress and peered under it. Nothing. I lifted the foot of the mattress, then the other side. Bingo.

Feeling triumphant, I pulled out a small book about three by five inches that bore a striking similarity to the book Daniel had stolen the day I'd chased him through town. I'd lay odds it was the exact same book. When I opened it, my excitement quickly waned. The words inside were handwritten and in a different language.

I tucked the book into the waistband of my jeans and smoothed out my shirt to make sure the bulge wasn't obvious. It wasn't that I didn't trust Marty, but I wasn't ready to let him in on the entire investigation.

After locking the door behind me, I sent Marty a text to say I'd catch up with him later.

Bobbie wouldn't be happy that I'd searched Daniel's house, but I had to make her understand. There was something sinister going on having to do with the bookshop, Jane Jones, Daniel Holland, and maybe others.

Bernard would be on my side. I was sure of it. I stuck

my hand in my pocket, pulled out Bobbie's list, and groaned. Next stop—The General Store.

After Bobbie unpacked the three bags of groceries I brought home, I suggested we visit Arrow Investigations, hoping she didn't ask why. I wanted Bernard for backup when I told Bobbie I'd taken up breaking and entering.

We were soon seated in our usual spot across from Bernard at his desk with Kit curled up on Bobbie's lap. I might not have bothered confiding in Bernard if I'd known I'd be getting a lecture.

"When I gave you the address, I never thought you'd break in. You could have been arrested. Or worse." Bernard sounded crankier than I'd seen him.

"But I wasn't." I ought to get some credit for that.

"Your grandmother and I told you to stay out of this investigation."

"But I am involved." I did my best not to sound like a petulant child, but he and Bobbie were being unreasonable. "And besides, what did you think I was going to do with Holland's address? Go over and throw a tea party on the lawn?"

"Listen to Bernard, dear." Bobbie patted my arm. "You don't have the training that he and I have."

"I don't want you involved either," Bernard told Bobbie. "It's much too dangerous."

Bobbie's frown lines deepened. "But—"

"One person is dead, and your granddaughter was injected with a powerful drug."

"But—"

"No buts."

They glared at each other in silence. I stood, and Bernard gave me a smug look. Perhaps he thought I'd given up the fight, but I had a trick up my sleeve, or rather down my pants. I pulled the book from my jeans.

"I guess I should turn this over to the police, then."

"What—" Bernard sputtered, unable to say anything other than, "Is that...?"

"This, I believe..." I held up the journal so he and Bobbie could get a good look. "...is the book that Daniel stole from Birch Street Bookshop."

Bobbie gasped.

"But since you don't want Bobbie or me involved," I continued, "then I guess I'll have to turn it over to the proper authorities." That was a bluff. No way was I giving the book to Wallenthorp.

"Let me have a look at that." Bernard reached out his hand eagerly.

"Say please..." I waggled the book just out of his reach

Bernard closed his eyes in frustration. "Please, Whitley."

"Give him the book already," Bobbie said. "The suspense is killing me."

"Fine." I held it out to Bernard, who snatched it from me. "You won't be able to read it, anyway."

He flipped through the pages, then narrowed his eyes at me. "Where'd you find this?"

"Daniel had hidden it under his mattress. Do you know what language it's in?"

He flipped a few more pages before shaking his head and scowling. "I'm guessing it's in English."

"Huh?" That made no sense. "I'll have you know I'm very good at reading English and that," I pointed at the book, "is gibberish."

"I'm sure it looks like gibberish, but I suspect it's written in code." He flipped a few more pages. "It appears to be old, so that's encouraging."

"It is?"

"Ciphers have become much more sophisticated over the past several decades. They're nearly impossible to break without knowing the algorithm used to encode them." He perused another page. "I'd go to the library if I were you."

"Can't I find the same information online?"

"I'm not suggesting you go to the library for a book. I'm suggesting you meet with a person: Eleanor Thorne."

"Who's she?" I asked.

"Ms. Thorne is a linguistics expert, and I'm pretty sure she can help you decode it. Would you like me to call and set up an appointment with her?"

"Why not? Sounds like fun." I'd gotten so good at slipping in sarcastic comments that Bernard seemed to think I meant it. I expected the visit to be anything but fun, but if I learned why the thief had stolen the book, it would be worth it.

Eleanor Thorne would meet with me at one p.m., which gave me about an hour to kill. I made a copy of the journal's pages, so the original could stay in the office safe, while Bobbie and Bernard whispered in the corner. It sounded like Bobbie worried we'd get in hot water for not turning the journal over to the police. Bernard told her that was unlikely since they'd already searched the house before I entered it.

"Besides," I overheard him say, "If they had found it, it would be gathering dust in an evidence locker. At least this way, we might actually learn something from it."

After dropping Bobbie and Kit off at home, I stopped off at the General Store for a sub sandwich. I ate in my car, then drove to the library.

The original library, which was housed in an old inn, burned down during the Pinecrest fire of 1998. An old school bus was converted to a bookmobile until finally the city got the funds to buy and remodel the defunct Quick N' Save building next to the post office.

The commercial space got a makeover, including a "modern" exterior like nothing the town had seen. It caused a lot of commotion and outcry among the community, but after all that settled down, the town decided they liked the new library after all.

I'd never been inside, but didn't expect much. I was pleasantly surprised to see what the designer had done with the interior, having raised the roof at least ten feet and installing skylights that gave the library a bright open ambiance.

A young woman sat behind a low counter to my left.

"I'm here to see Eleanor Thorne," I said in my best library voice. "She's expecting me."

According to Bernard, who'd called ahead on my

behalf, Eleanor Thorne was a retired linguistics professor who spoke eighteen languages fluently and had a special interest in ciphers.

Eleanor stood nearly six feet tall, not including the bun on top of her head that had only partially tamed her white mane. She wore an unfashionable midi length skirt, a tweed jacket, and sturdy black shoes.

The woman peered at me through thick glasses before shaking my hand firmly. "I'm Eleanor Thorne." Her voice was surprisingly strong and steady.

I followed her to a small study room with glass windows, which she unlocked. As I took a seat across from her at the kids-sized round table, I studied her face which remained nearly unwrinkled. It was as if she were cosplaying as an older, respected academic. Maybe she tried to appear older on purpose to gain the respect of her colleagues and students. I didn't judge.

She pulled a small notebook out of her jacket pocket. "The man who called..." She checked her notes. "Mr. Fernsby. He said you found an interesting journal or diary, perhaps written in code. May I see it?"

"I didn't bring it with me," I told her. "But I copied a couple of pages."

I pulled the folded sheets out of my pocket and smoothed them out before handing them across the table.

After she inspected them carefully, she pulled a pencil from behind her ear and became quickly engrossed, scribbling in a notebook.

When she looked up, she smiled for the first time. "This is a coded diary, as I suppose you might have guessed. It appears to be quite old. It wasn't unusual for young girls, especially teenagers, to write in code. Is the entire book written this way?"

"Yes, I think so."

"That's a bit unusual since, as you might imagine, it's quite tedious and time consuming to do. Often girls would only use code to hide the 'naughty bits'." Eleanor used air quotes to highlight those last words.

"How interesting." What I really felt was disappointment. It didn't seem likely that a teenager's diary, with or without 'naughty bits' would have anything to do with Daniel's death or the attack on me.

"Where did you find the diary?"

"I'd rather not say, if you don't mind."

A shadow of displeasure flickered in her eyes before she resumed her former pleasant expression. "I'm quite fascinated with local history and if this was written by one of the young ladies in the original colony, it might add to our knowledge about the early days of Arrow Springs. You know that some people claim that our founder, Franklin Norvelt, was a cult leader. This diary might even belong to one of his daughters."

"Is that so?" I stood to go. "I won't take up any more of your time."

"Not at all. I'd love to take the diary off your hands if you'd like to donate it. I could translate the entire text before turning it over to the historical society."

"Thanks, I'll think it over." I reached for the copies, which she reluctantly handed back to me.

"I doubt it would have much monetary value, but I'd be happy to talk to the historical society and see what they'd be willing to offer for it. You can bring it by anytime. I'm here weekdays from ten to six."

"Thanks." My spidey sense began to tingle. Why did she want the diary if it was nothing more than a teenager's puberty-fueled secrets? "I'll definitely let you know."

When I figure out why you want it so badly.

Chapter Fifteen

My phone buzzed, and I ignored it until I got back in my car.

The message read: *Please stop by the bookshop.* I didn't recognize the number.

Who's this? I typed.

Jane Jones.

I stared at the message, wondering if I should trust the sender, if it even was Jane Jones. Was she to be trusted? I considered asking what she wanted, but figured, hey, it's just a bookstore.

Still, maybe better to tell someone where I was. My grandmother hardly ever looked at her text messages, so I called the land line and left her a message. Just in case.

When I pulled up in front of the bookshop, there were other cars out front, so I let my guard down a bit. Herman lurked by the bushes. A second look told me he was holding hedge trimmers—so not actually lurking. Still, after spotting me, he turned and walked in the opposite direction. *Sheesh.* You'd think he'd have gotten over me not going to the Olympics. I had.

Jane waited for me by the register. After greeting me with a nod and a slight smile, she maneuvered her wheelchair through the aisles and toward the back of the shop and I followed.

We reached the back wall where we stood facing floor to ceiling bookshelves.

"Would you grab that red book for me?" She pointed to a volume titled *The Complete Works of Lewis Carroll.*

I had no idea what game she was playing, but for now, I went along. When I pulled the book from its spot, the entire bookcase slid to the side, exposing an elevator.

"Wow." I should have expected an elevator, especially with the owner's limited mobility. "That's pretty cool."

When the doors opened and we entered, Jane pushed the button for the second floor. "The hidden elevator is an attraction on its own, but it tends to bring in more curiosity seekers than book buyers."

The elevator lurched and slowly began its climb. Another lurch, and the doors opened. We exited into an expansive room with a large oval table surrounded by chairs. Seated there were three people I'd met before.

Jane made her way to the table and gestured to the others. "Whitley Leland, meet the members of the Society for Ancient Wisdom."

The Society for Ancient Wisdom, as Jane explained it, were caretakers of a repository of ancient texts that they scoured through, searching for important knowledge that had been lost to time.

"Allow me to introduce the members. First, you may have met—"

"Hello, Mrs. Nettle." She didn't seem to fit in with the others, with her baggy cat-themed sweatshirt.

"Nice to see you," Mrs. Nettle said with a nod.

"Nora Nettle," Jane said, "is an expert in other-species communication."

"You mean she talks to cats?" I guessed.

Mrs. Nettle frowned. "And other species. Raccoons are very chatty."

"I see." I began to wonder about Jane's society, but I chose to withhold judgment until I'd met the others.

"And this is Dr. Victor Zhang."

Dr. Zhang was a retired archeology professor who sometimes gave lectures at the community center. Bobbie had talked me into going with her once, but after I fell asleep halfway through, she never asked me again.

"Dr. Zhang just returned two days ago from several weeks abroad visiting locations where he believes prehistoric megalithic structures once stood."

"Like Stonehenge?" I asked.

Zhang sounded snooty, but that might have been his British accent. "Stonehenge is one of the least interesting of the monuments. Others have been discovered around the world, and even more were lost to time, but I've been extrapolating their locations by the use of a program I've developed. The implications for society are unquantifiable."

Jane thankfully stopped him, since I didn't understand

half of what he said. "Thank you, Victor." She moved to the far end of the table where a woman with a frizzy white bun watched me with keen eyes.

"Eleanor Thorne," I said. "We meet again."

"Yes, Eleanor mentioned you consulted with her. Did she mention she speaks eighteen languages fluently and can read several more?" Jane asked. "In addition, it's not common knowledge, but Eleanor spent many years involved in the intelligence community."

"Is that what we call universities now? There's plenty of intelligent people that never went to college. I heard that Einstein dropped out of high school. Did you know that?"

"I was referring to intelligence agencies that work to secure our national security."

"Yeah, I was just kidding," I bluffed.

"That's how I first met Eleanor, in fact. We worked together in the—"

"You are a spy!" I blurted out. "Kelvin was right."

"I was not a spy." Jane shook her head condescendingly. "I gathered and organized information for other agencies to keep them informed on what our adversaries were planning. Eleanor and I worked behind the scenes, but it was nonetheless vital to keeping our country and its citizens safe."

"Boy, wait until I tell Bobbie that Kelvin was right. She didn't believe him. I mean, I didn't believe him either, but he sure did seem convinced that something was going on over here."

"You can't tell your grandmother."

"Oh right. I suppose your society is doing top secret

work to protect the U S of A. Can't let anyone find out what you're up to, right?" I wasn't sure what to make of the blank stare she fixed me with. "What does your society do exactly?"

"We are searching for a portal to other dimensions."

"Huh?"

Before I could ask what the heck she was talking about, the elevator door opened behind us.

A voice cheerily said, "Sorry I'm late. What did I miss?" Marty stopped when he saw me. "Oh. Hi, Whitley."

We stared at each other for several seconds.

I decided to deal with Marty later and turned back to Jane. "Did you say you're looking for a portal to other dimensions?" I wanted to make sure I'd heard her correctly. "Like where?"

Mrs. Nettle piped up. "That's the question, isn't it?"

"We won't find out until we get there," Victor added. "We might find alternate realities, alien civilizations, or a doorway into the future."

"Thanks to Victor's help," Jane said, "I was able to locate the intersection of several key ley lines—"

"Ley lines?" I interrupted.

"Ley lines connect ancient sites around the world, both manmade and natural. They carry rivers of energy around the globe, resulting in concentrated energy where they converge, like right here."

"Right here?" I asked dubiously. "In Arrow Springs?"

"Right here under this bookshop."

I looked from one face to the next, thinking perhaps I was being pranked, but they all gazed back at me earnestly, except for Marty, who gave me a sheepish smile.

"This is all very interesting." I hoped I sounded convincing, since I didn't want it to be too obvious I thought they were off their rockers. "So, why did you invite me here?"

"Have a seat." Marty stood and pulled out a chair next to him.

"Thanks, I'll stand." I gave him a look meant to communicate how pissed off I was for keeping this a secret from me.

"You've been poking around," Jane said. "Asking questions."

"Yeah?" I didn't try to hide my indignation. "I got attacked in the basement of this building. And then left unconscious in a locked room. Was it one of you that did that to me?"

Jane appeared appropriately shocked. "Don't be ridiculous. Why would any of us do that?"

"To give you time to move the body and throw it in the lake."

Jane chuckled. "That's a ridiculous theory. We were meeting in the back room of Purrs and Pours at the time you were attacked, except for Victor, of course, who was still out of the country. When Mrs. Nettle found you in the alley, the meeting had just broken up. We can all vouch for each other."

I looked from Eleanor to Victor to Mrs. Nettle to Marty before returning my gaze to Jane. Not one of them flinched. Jane was either telling the truth or they were all in on it together, including Marty.

"Fine. Clam up." I hoped I sounded more convincing than I felt. "I'm going to find out who drugged me and locked me in that room."

"Well, we can't stop you," Mrs. Nettle said.

Jane touched my arm. "I'll show you out."

I guessed that meant I was being dismissed. Fine by me. Jane and I rode the elevator in silence. When it reached the first floor, the doors remained closed.

Jane turned to me. "Nora is right. We can't stop you from investigating. But I have one request of you."

"What is that?" I asked impatiently. Closed spaces made me uncomfortable.

"I would like you to swear to keep what you've learned about the Society a secret and not share it with anyone—not even your grandmother."

"I don't keep secrets from Bobbie." The stuffy air began to close in on me. "Is it warm in here?"

"I need you to keep this one."

I gave a one-shoulder shrug. "And if I don't?"

"I hoped you wouldn't be difficult. The others said you would be, but I said, 'No, she's a bright young woman, she'll understand.'"

She finally flipped a switch that opened the doors, and I hurried out, taking a deep breath of fresh air. She led me halfway down an aisle and came to a stop.

She turned her wheelchair to face me. "You will keep our secret."

I wasn't about to let her push me around. "You are in no position to make demands of me."

"Oh, but I am." The hint of a smile formed on her lips. "The society has obtained information about you and your family that is not public knowledge."

"You were snooping into my life?" I felt my shoulders tense the way they did when I was about to lose my temper. I forced myself to speak evenly and calmly. "That's okay. I have nothing to hide."

"You don't, but your family is a different story. I've had long conversations with the other members, and I've been outvoted. If need be, they will use the information to keep you in line."

My eyes narrowed. "What do you mean, 'use the information'?"

"I'm guessing you wouldn't want your grandfather to find out where your parents are."

Now I was lost. "I have no idea what you're talking about. My grandfather is dead. And my parents are in Beverly Hills. It's not a secret."

"I meant your birth father's father." She paused to let that sink in. "What would he do if he found out he had a granddaughter living right here in Arrow Springs?"

Isabella's words came back to me. "I am hoping to surprise him with a person. His granddaughter."

"My aunt already knows about me. It's only a matter of time before she tells him."

"In that case, I hope they haven't told you where Julia and Alejandro are living now or the new names they've been given."

I didn't want to let on how little I knew, so I said simply, "I haven't seen them since I was an infant, but I'm guessing your contacts have already filled you in on the whole sad story."

"I'm sorry, Whit. I hoped it wouldn't come to this, but after the years of work we've done on this project, we can't risk anyone else finding out about it."

"What about the dead guy? Daniel? Did he find out your secret? Is that why you killed him?"

My words seemed to knock the wind out of her, and it took her a moment to speak. "I didn't kill anyone. I wouldn't... I never could."

"If you didn't kill him, then it was one of the people upstairs. You know that, right?"

It took her a moment longer than it should have for her to reply. "That's not possible. We were all together at the time that man was killed."

"Okay, here's the deal." I didn't care if she agreed or not. Either way, I was going to be the one to call the shots. "I'm telling Bobbie and Bernard Fernsby everything I know." I held up a hand to keep her from objecting. "Just the two of them. They'll keep your secret."

"That's not acceptable."

"I don't care." There was no way I was keeping anything secret from Bobbie. Not after all we'd been through. "It's not negotiable. You can tell your friends upstairs about our deal or not. That's up to you. And if you want the three of us to keep your secret, I suggest you hire Arrow Investigations to solve Daniel's murder."

She raised an eyebrow. "Oh, you do?"

"Bobbie, Bernard and I are going to find out who murdered Daniel and who attacked me and locked me in the storage room with your help or not. I have a feeling you have information that will help us with that investigation."

Her expression didn't change, but she said, "Possibly."

"The only way to guarantee that what we learn about you, specifically, stays confidential, is if you hire us to investigate. You understand, of course, that confidentiality doesn't include illegal acts."

"Of course."

She seemed to be going along with my scheme, so I kept going. "Stop by Arrow Investigations tomorrow morning, say ten a.m.?"

After a long hesitation, she said, "I'll be there."

The moment I stepped outside into the bright sun, my phone buzzed.

Hey. It was from Marty.

I stared at the message, then put my phone back in my pocket. It buzzed again, but I ignored it. If he wanted to apologize for forgetting to mention that he was in some sort of secret society with Jane and her wacky friends, he'd have to wait.

By the time I got home, it had buzzed a few more times. A quick look told me they were all from Marty.

Can we talk?

Are you mad at me?

I can explain

Please answer

Sorry. I should have told you.

He had that last one right.

I found Bobbie in the backyard watering the shrubbery surrounding the dead lawn, while Kit tried to bite the water coming out of the hose. Bobbie's eyes got wider and wider as I told her everything that had happened since I'd dropped her off at home earlier that day.

"Mrs. Nettle thinks she can talk to cats?"

"And raccoons, apparently. I didn't get a chance to ask her what sort of things they like to talk about. Probably where the best trash cans are."

"And she expects us to keep her wacky 'Society' a secret?"

"She does. And we will."

My tone of voice must have told her how serious I was, because her eyebrows drew together in a frown. "We will?"

I didn't want to tell her the rest, but I needed her to know how serious this was. "Did you know that Julia and Alejandro are in the witness protection program?"

She barely reacted to this news. "I didn't know." After a long pause, she added, "But I suspected."

I'd have to add that to all the other things she hadn't told me about my birth parents. "According to Jane, at least one member of her group is willing to use that information if their secret gets out."

"Use it? How?"

"I'm guessing telling the bad guys where to find them." The worst of all the bad guys being my own grandfather, apparently.

Bobbie turned the hose off, and Kit and I followed her inside. I grabbed the dog and a towel to wipe off her muddy paws, but most of the mud ended up on me.

Bobbie started a new pot of coffee. "They would do that to us just to keep their silly society a secret? Does she think anyone in town cares? It's ridiculous."

I sat down at the kitchen table to wait for the pot to brew. "But I had another idea. What if they're really looking for something more tangible?"

"Like what?"

"Not sure. Buried treasure?"

Chapter Sixteen

The next morning, I went on a run to burn off the calories I'd been indulging in. Running also helped me think. It always surprised me how much my thoughts tended to organize themselves into sensible theories while my feet pounded against the ground and my conscious brain focused on not stepping on a rock or tripping over a tree root.

The journal had to be important, unless Daniel had stolen it by mistake. That was a possibility, since he'd gone back to the bookshop a second time. Had he pinched the wrong book?

Or had he gone back to look for buried treasure?

After I showered, Bobbie and I stopped by Bernard's favorite donut shop on the way to his office. We arrived half an hour before Jane was due.

"A buried treasure isn't that wild of an idea," he said once I'd finished. "Franklin Norvelt made his fortune during the gold rush. It's how he funded his utopian community and why it fell apart after his death. Once they incorporated as Arrow Springs, they were able to lure in other investors."

"He was a gold miner?"

"He started out that way, and had some success, but he really made it big by selling picks and shovels and other supplies to the next wave of miners who arrived. Most of them paid him in gold or silver. California didn't become a U.S. state until 1850, and in those early years, most people didn't trust paper money."

"Thanks for the history lesson, but can we get back to the treasure?"

Bobbie lightly smacked my arm, but Bernard chuckled, used to my impatience by now. "There's a legend that's been around since I was a kid, that when Norvelt died, no one found his gold stash because he'd buried it."

"The bookstore has a plaque by the front door that says it's a historical building. I don't remember what year—"

Bobbie interrupted me with, "1858."

"Maybe that was Norvelt's house, and he buried the gold under the floorboards. Maybe that's what Jane and their society are looking for."

Bernard shook his head. "My grandfather's family moved to Arrow Springs when he was just a kid. He told me lots of stories he heard about the old days before and after the city incorporated. According to him, after Norvelt died, they went through every inch of his house, practically tearing it apart looking for the gold. They even dug up the backyard. His fortune, if there was anything left, was never found."

"His daughters were left penniless?"

"Daughters?" Bernard gave me a quizzical look. "He never had daughters, but he did have two sons. As I recall, they inherited his land and other assets. I'm sure they made out just fine."

"He didn't have any daughters? Were there other Norvelts?"

"His sons might have had daughters. I don't recall. But they were quite young when Norvelt died."

"Can we talk about Jane Jones before she arrives?" Bernard asked. "Why is she hiring me—"

"Us," I corrected.

He took a moment to consider that. "All right. Why is she hiring us?"

"So we don't blab. You know, client privilege."

"Whitley." Bernard shook his head slowly. "That only works for lawyers."

"And priests," Bobbie added.

"Communications between private investigators and their clients are not protected under the law."

"Oh." What seemed like a good idea at the time was becoming less so. "She doesn't need to know that, does she?"

Bernard looked at Bobbie and back at me. "What exactly did you tell Jane?"

"Never mind," Bobbie said. "Let's wait until she gets here and see what she expects."

A knock from outside was followed by the creak of the door as it opened and Jane's voice calling out, "Hello?"

Bobbie hurried into the front room and escorted her into Bernard's office. At Bobbie's non-verbal signal, I swung my chair over to the side of the desk to make room for Jane's wheelchair. That allowed me to keep an eye on Jane during the interview. I wasn't sure if I should trust her or not, but I leaned toward not.

Bernard and Jane exchanged introductions, and Bobbie shook her hand with a welcoming smile. I gave her a nod.

Bernard began by saying that I'd brought them up to speed on what I'd learned the previous day. "And I understand you'd like to hire us to find out who murdered Daniel Holland."

Jane glanced over at me before answering. "Yes. I've been assured you'll keep any information I share with you about myself and the other members of the Society confidential."

"My reputation and that of Arrow Investigations depends on my discretion. I won't share any information without your permission unless required by law. In order to maintain the level of discretion you're requesting, I recommend that we avoid all written communication, including emails. The three of us will only take notes if necessary."

"And why is that?" Jane asked.

"Verbal communication is not discoverable. That means we aren't required to share what we've discussed with prosecutors or law enforcement. If Daniel's killer were arrested and brought to trial, any written records could be subpoenaed."

Jane's frown softened into something of a smile. "I see. So, confidentiality isn't exactly guaranteed, but..."

"But there's no reason that any information other than evidence of a crime will come out."

"Exactly."

"Jane," Bobbie began tentatively, "why do you want to keep your society secret? Are you doing anything illegal?"

"No, of course not. But we are on the brink of a major discovery. The longer we can keep our activities out of the public eye, the more likely we'll be able to accomplish our mission. And if we fail, which I have to admit is a possibility, then I'd rather fail privately."

"Do you think Daniel Holland was interested in your mission, as you call it?"

"Perhaps. Why else was he sneaking around at my bookstore? And before you ask, I have no idea who killed him. Honestly, the only reason I care about his murder is the way it affects our plans. I'm sorry if that sounds cold, but I never knew the man, after all. The last thing we need is the police poking around and asking too many questions. Whitley made me realize that the sooner someone is arrested for the murder, the sooner the police will stop bothering us."

Bernard handed Jane a contract and suggested she review it. Once it was signed, Bernard began his interview. I figured he called it that because it sounded better than interrogation.

"I've reviewed the police report about Daniel's death," Bernard said. "While certain details were redacted in order to not compromise the investigation and any future court case, what we have learned is that Daniel Holland was killed sometime on Sunday, late morning or early afternoon. It was around noon that Whitley," he gestured to me, "found him in the basement of your bookshop, unconscious or perhaps already deceased."

"There wasn't any pulse, and he felt sort of cold." The memory made me shiver. "And then someone jumped me."

"We'll get to that shortly." Bernard turned his attention back to Jane. "Whitley believes that one of the members of your society may have been responsible for Holland's death. I understand you claim you were all together off site at the time."

"We were having a meeting at Purrs and Pours when Whitley broke into my bookshop."

"Hey," I objected. "I didn't break in. The door was unlocked. Kelvin thought someone might be in trouble or something." I chose not to mention that he'd bugged her shop.

"That man," Jane huffed. "What is his obsession with me? Always watching me through binoculars. It's creepy."

"He says you're a spy and turns out he was right."

"I worked for an intelligence agency, which doesn't make me a spy."

"Let's get back to the subject at hand, shall we?" Bobbie suggested. "What time did you and the others meet? And where?"

"We met in the back room of Purrs and Pours," Jane said. "Shortly after eleven."

"And why didn't you meet at the bookshop?" I asked.

"After all, you have that nice big room on the second floor."

"Whitley," Bobbie said. "Would you please let her give her account? There will be plenty of time for questions after she's done."

I sank down in my chair and crossed my arms, annoyed and a little embarrassed to be chastised by my grandmother.

Jane resumed her story. "I arrived at the cat café first. Nora, Mrs. Nettle, that is, was serving customers in the café. Shortly after that, the other members arrived."

"Including Martin Blackwood?" Bernard asked. "He's also a member, correct?"

"Martin brought coffee for everyone from Sugar Buns. Mrs. Nettle didn't like that. She asked him what was wrong with her coffee, and they got into a little tiff."

"And why didn't you meet in the bookshop?" Bernard asked, giving me a nod.

"Herman had been pestering me to join the book club for months."

"Herman?" I asked before I could stop myself. "The old guy?"

"He works for me part time, helping with odd jobs. There's a lot he can't do at his age, but it's not easy to find help in the off season, and he's handy enough."

"You were saying about the book club?" Bernard prompted her.

"It's a front for the society. It allows us to meet privately without having to explain what we're doing. Herman wanted to join, but I told him we weren't accepting new members. Then Victor was on an extended leave, and Herman wanted to take his spot. I told him the club was taking a hiatus. If we'd met at the bookshop, he'd have thought I'd been lying to him."

"You were lying to him." I figured I was the best one to say it out loud.

Jane shot me a glare. "About a book club. A little white lie."

As far as I was concerned, someone who could easily tell a "little white lie" and maintain that lie for a period of months was capable of deceiving them about something bigger, like a secret society. Or a murder.

I kept that thought to myself, and instead asked, "How do we know Herman didn't kill Daniel?"

Jane snickered. "Have you met Herman? He must be eighty years old if he's a day."

Bernard cleared his throat as a sign he wanted to get back on track. "Daniel Holland stole a book from your bookshop on Saturday. Why?"

She gave him a bored look, as if already tired of answering questions. "I've asked myself that question. If I knew which book he took, I might have a better answer for you. The cabinet he broke into had a collection of old journals. Some of them might have belonged to Franklin Norvelt and his family, so I'd asked Eleanor to ascertain their value, both monetary and historical."

"And to learn about the portal's location?" I asked.

Her eyes darted to me, her surprise obvious, although she did her best to cover it up. "We theorized that Norvelt knew about this area's special properties, and that's why he chose to settle here. But Eleanor hasn't found anything useful so far."

"Do you have an attorney?" Bernard asked.

"I have someone I consult for business matters." Jane pressed her lips together tightly. "Are you saying I need a lawyer? I had nothing to do with the thief's death."

"Of course not," Bernard said. "But the police arrest innocent people all the time. Usually, they are freed quickly, but not always. It's best to be prepared."

"Thank you." Jane pulled her wheelchair back from the desk, appearing more irritated than grateful. "I'll consider it."

Chapter Seventeen

After Jane left, we discussed our game plan. Bernard would do a background check on all the society members.

"Including Jane, right?" I asked, wanting to make sure we covered all our bases.

"Most definitely, including Jane."

Meanwhile, Bobbie would visit Mrs. Nettle, while Bernard contacted Victor Zhang. We wanted to see if their stories lined up.

Bobbie stood, her purse over one arm. "If we confirm they were all together at Purrs and Pours when Whitley was attacked, we'll have to widen our net."

"What if they met at Purrs and Pours after Daniel was killed?" I asked. "He might have been dead for a while when I found him."

Bernard opened his file and shuffled through some papers. "The estimated time of death from the Medical

Examiner supports that possibility. But if that's the case, who attacked you?"

"An accomplice?" It was the best idea I could come up with. "Or some kind of cleaner, like the mob has. You call them up and they take care of things."

"I doubt Jane has someone like that in her Rolodex," Bobbie said.

"What's a Rolodex?"

"Never mind." Bobbie tapped her foot. "Are you coming with me?"

I shook my head. "I'm going to go talk to Marty."

"Marty?" Bernard asked. "You mean Martin Blackwood?"

"They've become friendly," Bobbie explained, as if I couldn't speak for myself.

Bernard's jaw dropped open. "You've become friendly with Martin Blackwood?"

"You say that as if it were the oddest thing you've heard all day when you just found out there's a society right here in town looking for a portal to other worlds."

"The thing is... he's sort of a recluse." Bernard paused. "Scratch that. He's a total recluse."

"Yeah, he told me that."

"The few times I've seen him out and about, he was wearing a hat with his jacket turned up like he didn't want anyone to talk to him."

I grinned. "Maybe my sparkling personality won him over."

Bobbie stifled a snicker. "Yes, dear. That must be it."

My text to Marty was simple and to the point: *OK let's meet.*

Him: *P&P?*

Me: *Ugh. Anywhere but*

Him: *Crystal Creek Park?*

Me: *Give me 30.*

Kit danced around me as I put on my shoes, biting at the laces while I tried to tie them.

"Knock it off or I'll leave you behind." She jumped a few times like a pogo stick. "Sit!" She tilted her head as if she didn't understand, but I knew better. She only obeyed when she wanted. I could relate.

I snapped on her leash, called out goodbye to Bobbie, and headed down the hill. First stop was Sugarbuns for cinnamon rolls and cappuccinos.

"Hey Mitsy," I called out as I entered.

Her smile widened when she saw Kit. "I got something for her. Is it okay if I give her a treat?"

At the word "treat," Kit's ears perked up, and she stood on her hind legs with her tongue hanging out of her mouth.

"It's okay with me," I said. "But she should earn it. How about a backflip for your favorite baker?"

Kit gave me a questioning look before refocusing her attention on Mitsy.

"Fine, I'll go first." I got into position and made sure I had enough room before executing a tight, clean backflip, landing perfectly on my feet.

Mitsy clapped. "That was amazing."

"Your turn," I said to Kit.

She cocked her head to one side as if she didn't understand, but she sat still waiting for my command.

"If you want the perk, you gotta do the work." I pointed at her, and as I jerked my hand up, I said, "Flip."

Kit performed a perfect backflip, even better than mine, if I was being honest.

"Show off," I grumbled as Mitsy lavished praise on the little mutt.

"Good thing you don't have a line of customers right now," I said.

"That's one of my favorite things about this job. It's super busy in the morning for like three hours, then it's totally dead. If I want, I can read or watch videos the rest of the day."

"You ever read Martin Blackwood's books?"

"I tried, but it was pretty heavy." She made a sour face. "I hate war."

"I don't think anyone likes it."

She wrinkled her nose. "Then why do we always have them? Someone must think war is a good thing."

"You ever meet Marty?"

"Oh sure." Her smile returned. "It's funny. He wears disguises all the time, so he doesn't get recognized. In the winter, it's a hoodie and sunglasses. Like who wears sunglasses when the sun's not out?"

I figured that was a rhetorical question, but I answered it anyway. "Half the people in L.A."

"Oh, right. Movie stars."

"And people who want people to think they're movie stars. They walk around in their designer sweats and perfect hair and pretend they don't want to be noticed. If you really wanted to be ignored, all you have to do is be average like me and no one takes a second look."

Mitsy snickered. "You? Average? Have you even met yourself?"

I let that comment slide. "So, Marty's disguises don't fool anyone, huh?"

"They fool plenty of people. Not me, though."

"Oh, right." Mitsy's internal facial recognition was better than any computer program.

Mitsy stood and brushed the hair off her apron. "How many cinnamon rolls today?"

"Two, and two cappuccinos."

"Just two cinnamon rolls? Don't tell me you're cutting back."

I patted my stomach. "Gotta stay in shape for my next stunt gig. If they would let the actresses get chubby, then I could too, but that's not gonna happen anytime soon."

"I feel bad for them, always having to starve themselves. But you don't do that."

"Not anymore. That's why I run." I reconsidered my order, counting on my fingers: Marty, me, two for Bobbie and me for breakfast tomorrow, and one in case of emergency. That made five. "I'll take six."

Kit wanted to sniff every bush and tree between Sugarbuns and the park, and I hoped Marty didn't mind waiting a bit. Crystal Creek Park was perfect if you didn't want to run into anyone, since it was nearly always empty. It was small and oddly shaped, like a rectangle drawn by a drunk person.

Marty sat on a bench with one arm draped casually over the back. He wore a U.S. Marines ball cap pulled low over his forehead, a zippered sweatshirt, and jeans. With the hat, I wouldn't have recognized him if I'd only seen the publicity photo on the back of his books.

Kit growled when she saw him until he leaned forward and held out his hand.

"Who's this?" he asked.

"This is my sidekick, Kit. She used to be a performing stunt dog before I got her."

Marty gave me a doubting look. "You're kidding."

"Nope. It's a long, long story involving dognapping and murder. I'll tell you about it some time."

Marty looked at Kit and back at me. "I never know when you're serious and when you're not." He patted the bench. "Want to hop up?"

Kit jumped onto the bench and curled up in his lap, making herself right at home.

Marty took off his hat and ruffled his hair the way he'd done the day I first met him at the police station. And then it hit me. He'd wanted me to recognize him that day. Why was that when he did his best to be unnoticed by pretty much everyone else?

I'd have to wait to figure that out.

I handed him his cappuccino. "Want a cinnamon roll?"

"No, thanks."

I sat next to him on the bench. "You're kidding right? Have you ever had one from Sugar Buns? By the way, Mitsy says 'hi.'"

He raised his eyebrows a fraction of an inch. "Are you trying to tell me my disguises aren't fooling anyone?"

"Nah, but they're not fooling Mitsy. Speaking of

fooling people, why didn't you tell me you were in cahoots with Jane and her weirdos?"

"They aren't weirdos. Well, maybe Nora, but she's probably harmless."

"You didn't answer my question."

He hung his head like a toddler who'd been caught stealing a cookie. "I was sworn to secrecy. Tell me the truth, if you'd known about the society, would you have been able to fake the surprise you showed when Jane introduced you to everyone? Especially me?"

"I can act. Sort of. Stunt work isn't all fight scenes and jumping out of windows." I tried to think of all the questions I wanted to ask and in what order, but instead, I blurted out, "Do you know who killed Daniel?"

He hadn't expected that question, judging by his expression. "No, I don't."

"Were you all really at the cat café when I was attacked? In case you don't remember, that was approximately noon on Sunday."

"Who told you about...?" he began. "Oh, right. Jane. That's great. She tells all of us to clam up and she goes blabbing to everyone—"

"She didn't blab. She hired Arrow Investigations to investigate the murder."

"She did? But..." he stopped speaking as if he'd thought better about what he'd been about to say.

"But what?"

"I figured Jane was the one who killed him."

Chapter Eighteen

When I was able to speak, I asked, "You think Jane murdered Daniel?"

"It seemed a logical conclusion. Daniel had stolen a book from her bookshop—a book that Jane says is worth little or nothing. Then he came back, but why? To steal some other worthless item? I don't buy it."

"But she's in a wheelchair."

"She could still hit someone over the head with a steel pipe," he said. "Or a bust of Shakespeare, for that matter. Besides, she's there whenever the bookshop is open. How did anyone get into the basement without her knowing it?"

"How do you know the cause of death was blunt trauma?" I asked.

"I wasn't sure. Until now."

I wagged a finger at him. "I don't like being played like that. If you want to know something, just ask."

He raised one eyebrow. "Would you have told me?"

"That's not the point. How about telling me about the

meeting on Sunday? What was so important everybody had to drop everything and meet up at the cat café?"

"Good question. Jane spent the first half hour complaining that Leo was late after he was the one who called the meeting."

"Leo? Leo who?"

"Leo Parrigan," he said.

"The pharmacist?" I jumped to my feet, and Kit lifted her head, her ears at attention. "He's in the society, too?"

"I thought you knew that."

"Oh, you did?" I was hopping mad now, fully aware that the whole park could hear me, but I didn't much care.

"Whit. Can you please..." Marty paused to nod at a man passing by who seemed concerned.

"Can I what? Calm down?" Kit seemed to sense how ticked off I was, because she climbed off Marty's lap. I scooped her up into my arms. "I'll calm down, but only because you're upsetting Kit."

"*I'm* upsetting her?"

"You obviously don't understand the ordeal I've been through." I kept my voice steady as I stroked Kit's fur. "Someone stuck a needle in my arm and filled me full of a powerful sedative. Then they locked me in a basement room where I could have died. Don't you think the town pharmacist might know something about that? And you, Jane, and the others forgot to mention that he was a member of your stupid society."

"I'm sorry, Whit. I assumed Jane told you." He reached for my hand, but I jerked it away.

Still fuming, I sat back down on the bench, holding Kit close and leaving a foot of empty space between us. "Tell me everything, and this time, don't leave anything out. You said Leo called the meeting, but then he was late?"

"The text came from his number." Marty pulled a phone out of his pocket that looked identical to one I had at age fifteen.

"The nineties are calling," I deadpanned. "They want their phone back."

He shrugged. "Jane got burner phones for all of us. She's very security conscious."

"If by that you mean she's borderline paranoid, I'd have to agree with you."

He pressed a few keys, then showed me the screen. "See? 'Important. Meet at P&P in 30.'"

"What time was that text?" I asked.

He took another look at the message. "Just after eleven."

I did my best to remember what Jane had told us. It would be a lot easier if Bernard had let me take notes. I closed my eyes and replayed her words in my mind.

"Jane never mentioned Leo—not that he called the meeting or that he was late." She hadn't told any of us that Leo was a member of the society. I doubted that was an innocent omission. "Why did he say he was late?"

"He told Jane he'd lost his burner phone and didn't even know about the meeting until she texted him on his personal phone. They had a very heated discussion, and then he stormed out. He said he had to get back to work, but the rest of us stayed a while longer."

"Who stayed behind? You, Jane, Mrs. Nettle, Eleanor, and Victor?"

"Victor was still out of the country."

I'd get Bernard to confirm that. "How much longer did you meet?"

"Until twelve-thirty or so. Jane got a text and said she needed to get back to the bookshop. She asked me to walk her back to her shop."

"What happened when you got to the bookshop? Did you go down to the basement?"

He nodded. "She asked me to wait while she checked whether Herman had brought up some boxes from the basement. He hadn't, so I moved them for her." He paused and his eyebrows drew together. "You might have been trapped down there while Jane had me doing her grunt work. I wonder if she knew." He stared off into the distance.

I tried to give him a moment to compose his thoughts, but impatience got the better of me. "Then what happened? After you moved the boxes."

"We talked for a while, and then Nora called. It must have been right after Nora took you to her cat café. Jane seemed agitated after she hung up the phone and said she had some work to do, so I left."

I wanted to believe him, but I needed to know if he was telling me the whole truth. "Are you sure it didn't happen the other way around? Jane found out I'd escaped from the basement room and called Mrs. Nettle?"

He stared at me intently. "You can trust me."

"Why should I?" I broke eye contact and watched a pair of squirrels chasing each other from tree to tree, not sure how to feel. "Because we shared a moment over a dying tree?" If Bobbie had been there, she would have scolded me for being mean, but the words left my mouth before I considered their impact.

"It's a nice tree," he said with a smile, as if trying to lighten the mood.

Kit spotted the squirrels and leaped off my lap, yanking at the leash to chase after them. After some stern words from me, she gave up and curled up on the grass.

"Wait." Something about the timing of that day was off, and I didn't like it. "Between the time Mrs. Nettle called Jane, and I arrived at the police station, it wasn't more than twenty or twenty-five minutes. You implied you'd been there all morning."

"I was there until I got the text about the meeting. And then, after I left Jane at the bookshop, I went back to the station."

"To see if I'd show up there?" I asked.

He winced. "I had no idea you'd be attacked, and no reason to expect you'd show up at the police station."

It all began to make sense, or at least some of it did. "That's why you made sure I recognized you." I could hardly breathe as the truth hit me. "You wanted to get closer to me to find out what was really going on. To get a scoop?"

"No, Whit." He leaned closer and spoke with such sincerity that I almost let my guard down. "I was at the police station to get a story, yes, but that's not why I wanted to get close to you."

I leaned back, folded my arms across my chest, and focused on the nearest tree. I wanted to cry or scream or slug him, but all that would have to wait.

"I went back to the bookshop later," he said. "After the

police questioned Jane, and we put two and two together, up to a point. At first, Jane thought you'd made the whole thing up—

or at least that's what she told me."

"She what?" I stared at him, dumbfounded.

"Remember, the body hadn't been found yet."

"Did you think I made it all up? Being attacked and locked in a room?"

Firmly and confidently, he said, "Not for a second."

"What's really going on, Marty?" I grew tired of all the lies and half-truths. "What is the Society really after? C'mon. Out with it."

Marty grimaced. "I don't know much more than you do."

"But there's something you're not telling me." I felt sure of it. "What happened to 'you can trust me'? You can't have it both ways. No wonder you're single."

"Ouch. That's a little close to home, Whit. Did you ever consider I might have a good reason for being single?"

"Because you have trust issues?"

"Because the last woman I fell in love with died in my arms."

What do you say when someone you might be interested in but who also might be a suspect in a murder investigation tells you their last girlfriend died in their arms?

"Oh, crap," was all I could come up with. "Sorry. There's something you should know about me. See, most people have thoughts up here," I pointed to the side of my head, "and there's some sort of filter that stops the inappropriate things from coming out of here." I pointed to my mouth. "I have what I'm pretty sure is a genetic defect. No filter."

He smiled. "I think that's why I like you, Whit." I must have given him a "you're kidding me," look because he added, "No, really. I don't have to be afraid of what you're not saying."

I considered that. "I'm pretty sure you're the first person who thinks that's a positive. And Bobbie, though she does scold me a lot."

I wondered if I should ask him about his dead girlfriend, but that would have to wait for another time. We had a murder to solve, and Marty was my best source of intel.

I cleared my throat. "What else can you tell me about Jane and the Society?"

He took a deep breath. "You didn't hear it from me." He paused dramatically. "Jane isn't looking for a dimensional portal to another world."

"No kidding."

His expression fell. "You already figured that out?"

"I didn't buy her story for a second. Jane's using the others to get what she wants, whatever that is."

"I was sure I was getting closer to the truth when Daniel Holland ended up dead. I might have asked Jane one too many questions. She closed up like a clam."

"No one would have even connected his murder to the bookshop if I hadn't gone over there."

"Your involvement was definitely inconvenient for the killer." He paused for a moment. "We know the body was in the basement at around noon when you were attacked, and it was gone when Jane and I came back after the meeting. Someone must have taken it to the lake, but who? An accomplice?"

"It would have to be someone strong."

"Not if there were two of them and they used a dolly. I bet a bookstore has one of those."

"The body disappears while everyone is conveniently in a meeting. Everyone except for Leo. He's strong enough, and his pharmacy carries propofol, one vial of which is conveniently missing." Excitement swelled in me, and I stood to leave, ready to tell Bernard and Bobbie what I'd learned.

Marty held up his index finger. "Other than the half hour or so he was with us at Purrs and Pours, he was at the pharmacy the rest of the day. He couldn't have done it."

I scoffed. "You're taking Leo's word for that?"

"I don't take anybody's word for anything. I talked to the pharmacy tech working with him that day, and he swears Leo didn't leave for more than thirty or forty-five minutes at most."

"Darn." All my excitement dissolved. "I'm going to have to check that alibi for myself."

Marty shoulders slumped. "You still don't trust me, do you?"

"Sorry, dude." I threw up my hands. "I can't take your word for everything just because I like you."

"You like me?" His smile widened. "I'll take it for now."

Chapter Nineteen

I hurried home, dragging Kit behind me as she tried to sniff every leaf of grass we passed. Since I wasn't supposed to write anything down, I wanted to tell Bobbie what I'd learned before I forgot any details, especially about Leo Parrigan being a member of Jane's Society.

When I got home, Bobbie poured me a cup of coffee and we put Bernard on speakerphone.

Once I'd told them everything I'd remembered, Bernard said, "I wonder why Jane didn't mention Leo."

"Maybe she didn't want us to connect her to the missing propanol," I suggested.

"Propofol," Bobbie said in a scolding tone. "Did you go to the pharmacy when you said you were running errands?"

"Yes," I said. "That was one of my errands. I'm surprised you or Bernard didn't ask about it. Or the police.

Sheesh." I pretended to be exasperated by their oversight. "I have to do everything around here."

I was met with silence, which was better than another lecture.

Bobbie spoke first. "Jane lied to us."

Bernard's voice came through the phone. "Or at the very least, she left out a lot of important information during her interview. That can happen with an unwilling participant."

I was to blame for that, I supposed. "I suspect she wouldn't care if someone got away with murder as long as her society stayed secret."

"Time to go back to the basics," Bernard said. "I'll confirm Parrigan's alibi."

"And can you find out when Victor Zhang came back to the U.S. from wherever he'd been? Supposedly he was out of town at the time of the murder."

"Will do," Bernard said. "Why don't the two of you go over each of the suspects, witnesses, and anyone connected to them?"

"Can we write it down?" I wasn't sure how I was supposed to keep all the information straight otherwise.

"Yes, but only in invisible ink." After a pause, Bernard added, "That was a joke."

"Oh. Ha ha."

"I haven't cashed Jane's check, and I don't plan to. From now on, when it comes to the Daniel Holland case, Arrow Investigations has one client."

"Who's that?" I asked.

"You, Whitley," Bernard said. "We are going to find out who attacked you."

Triple Shot

I ended the call and turned to Bobbie. "I'm a client," I said with a grin. "It's kinda fun."

"It's all fun and games until somebody gets murdered."

"Aw, why'd you have to go and spoil it?" I headed for the kitchen, where dark liquid sat at the bottom of the coffee carafe. "I think this calls for a fresh pot, don't you?"

Bobbie retrieved two spiral notebooks from the seemingly limitless supply in her office and handed me one. I tore out five sheets and laid them out on the dining room table. At the top of each page, I wrote the names Jane Jones, Victor Zhang, Leo Parrigan, Nora Nettle, and Eleanor Thorne. Next to Jane's name, I wrote, "Real name Marnie?"

"Don't forget Marty," Bobbie reminded me.

I reluctantly tore out a sixth sheet and labeled it Martin Blackwood.

Bobbie stared at the pages and sighed. "Do we know anything for sure?"

"We can make some pretty good assumptions." I tore off another sheet and labeled it The Society for Ancient Wisdom. "For instance, I don't believe for a second that Jane is looking for a portal into other dimensions."

"That did sound a bit fishy. I have to say Jane was very convincing when she told us. I wonder if she has acting experience."

"She's a former spy," I said. "Even if she had an office job, I'm sure she had to lie to a lot of people. I don't trust anything she says."

"Nor do I, dear."

We passed the sheets back and forth, reviewing each other's notes and adding others. After we'd written what little we knew about each of our suspects, I got up to refill our mugs. "Are we even making progress?"

"This is just the prep work." Bobbie took a sip of her coffee. "Next step is a timeline for Sunday when Daniel was murdered and you were attacked."

"Of course." I tore off a new sheet. First, I wrote the hours on the left side of the page starting with eleven a.m. when I went to see Kelvin, and ending with two in the afternoon, about the time Mrs. Nettle found me in the alley behind the bookshop.

"Daniel was murdered sometime after ten-thirty a.m. according to the M.E. And most likely before you found him in the basement."

I marked the time range on the sheet. "Whoever had Leo's phone called the meeting at three minutes after eleven. Marty showed me the text. Everyone has an alibi for when I was attacked—everyone but Leo, that is."

"But the murder could have happened between 10:30 and 11:00," Bobbie said. "We don't know where any of them were at that time, except perhaps Leo."

I tapped my pen against the table, trying to make sense of it all. "That would be a good reason to call a meeting and get their stories straight."

"And give themselves alibis if they needed one later. They wouldn't even have needed alibis if you hadn't shown up. That must have required some last-minute improvising."

I glanced at all our notes and the timeline. "Nothing about this seems planned to me."

"Maybe it was a crime of passion?" Bobbie said.

I considered the idea. "Why would Jane be that angry? Over a book?"

"It all comes down to what's in that book, doesn't it?" she asked. "Have you made any progress decoding it?"

"I haven't even started. To tell the truth, I have no idea where to start."

"You start at the beginning."

I winced, as I had a vision of how I'd be spending my evening.

"And," Bobbie added, "with a little help from your friends."

While Bobbie called her network of little old ladies—inviting them over for a working dinner—I searched my laptop for tips on decoding the journal. From what Eleanor had said, it was probably a simple substitution cipher where each letter of the alphabet was replaced by a different letter in a one-to-one relationship. The code might be changed for different pages, or it might not. We'd have to see.

Rosa arrived first, carrying something wrapped in aluminum foil. I took it into the kitchen where I was happy to learn it was a batch of freshly baked chocolate chip oatmeal cookies. I stuffed one in my mouth before returning to the dining room.

The next time the doorbell rang, it was the delivery guy from the Chinese restaurant. As he was leaving, Sunshine and Ralph came up the walk. They had finally come out as a couple.

Once everyone was settled at the table, and we'd set out the food, plates, and utensils, Bobbie explained what we wanted to accomplish.

"It's like real-life cryptograms." Rosa grinned. "How fun!"

Fun wouldn't be the first word I would have used. "What's a cryptogram?"

"They're my favorite word puzzles," Rosa explained. "The crossword puzzle books have them sometimes."

I couldn't imagine having a favorite word puzzle, but I was happy to have a sort of expert to help out. Rosa seemed positively excited when I handed her the copy I'd made of the first page. Since there were five of us and only one book, I went to the office to use Bobbie's multipurpose printer to copy the pages.

By the time I returned to the table, Rosa had created a key showing which letters to replace for which.

"If the code is different on different pages, you'll figure it out pretty quickly," she told us.

"How?" I asked.

"You'll end up with gibberish."

I made copies of the key, and Rosa, not surprisingly, was the first to complete decoding one of the pages. We listened as she read what the journal owner had written so many years earlier.

"It has been fifteen years since we established our community, driven by a shared dream of escaping the tumult of civilization and forging a new path amidst nature's bounty. As I sit here, overlooking the tranquil valley below, I am filled with a sense of pride and gratitude for what we have accomplished together.

"Yet amidst the tranquility of our haven, I cannot shake the gnawing concern that lingers at the back of my mind. With each passing day, I grow increasingly aware of my mortality and the uncertainty of what lies beyond. What will become of our community once I am no longer here to guide and protect it? Will our ideals endure, or will they wither away like leaves in the autumn breeze?"

Rosa paused and looked up expectantly.

"That doesn't sound like a teenage girl to me," I said. We were unlikely to come across any naughty bits if the rest of the journal was anything like what we'd just heard.

"Wait." Bobbie gave me a quizzical look. "Why did you think a young girl wrote it?"

"Eleanor Thorne told me the journal might have belonged to one of Norvelt's daughters."

"But he only had sons." Bobbie exchanged a look with me that told me we were thinking the same thing.

Eleanor Thorne lied.

Chapter Twenty

Sunshine and Ralph left, saying they had plans, but I figured they didn't find decoding the journal as much fun as Rosa did. It was just as well, since we weren't ready to share the real reason we were interested in the journal.

By this time, I'd found a website that allowed me to type in what I wanted decoded along with the key, so I was whizzing along even faster than Rosa.

As I reached the last few paragraphs, I began to think decoding the journal had been a complete waste of time. I scanned the words, glad to be close to the end.

I have devoted my life to nurturing this community, imparting upon its members the virtues of cooperation, self-sufficiency, and harmony with nature. But as I grow older, I realize that my time on this earth is finite, and I must confront the reality that I cannot remain at the helm forever. It pains me to contemplate the challenges my followers may face in my absence—the temptations of greed, the allure of power, the discord that can arise when unity falters.

When I read the next paragraph, I gasped.

Rosa looked up. "What is it?"

"Oh... I just realized I've reached the end, and I haven't learned anything to help us with our case." I stood. "Look at the time. I've got to go get ready. I've got a thing. Thanks for coming over, Rosa. You were a big help."

I picked up my laptop and the journal and went down the hall to my bedroom, Kit on my heels. She probably expected me to curl up for a nap, so she hopped up on the bed. To her disappointment, I set the laptop down and paced, hoping that Bobbie had gotten the hint.

A knock on the door was followed by Bobbie's voice. "Whitley?"

"Come in."

Kit jumped off the bed to greet Bobbie as if she hadn't seen her for days.

"I got rid of Rosa." Bobbie sat on my bed and Kit jumped in her lap, rolling on her back for belly rubs. "What did you find?"

"I'll read it to you." I cleared my throat and began. "I have entrusted the location of my remaining wealth to my most trusted confidant, knowing that when the time is right, destiny will guide its discovery into the hands of those who will use its riches for the betterment of all."

"His most trusted confidant?" Bobbie asked. "Who would that be?"

"No idea. Who do we know who's an expert on local history? Anyone?"

"I'll ask Bernard."

"Tell him I'm not going back to visit Eleanor Thorne," I called after her as she shuffled down the hall.

I stacked the pillows against the headboard and got comfy with Kit while I waited. When Bobbie returned, she wore a sheepish grin.

"He suggested one of us go to the library."

"To talk to Eleanor Thorne again?" I asked. "I hope you told him she's a great big fibber."

"I did, though I didn't use those exact words. He thinks it's worth talking to her again. He also suggested asking one of the librarians if they have a local history collection—many libraries do."

"You've always been much better at schmoozing people than me. Let me know if you find out anything useful."

Bobbie didn't budge from my doorway. I could feel her eyes on me, but I did my best to ignore my discomfort. I hoped she'd eventually give up.

I underestimated her persistence. "Fine. I'll go with you."

It was nearly five p.m., but since Eleanor Thorne had told me she was at the library every weekday until six, we didn't bother calling first.

The young woman at the front desk informed us Eleanor wasn't in.

"When do you expect her back?"

"I don't. She didn't come in at all today. She usually calls to let us know if she's taking a day off, but I suppose it slipped her mind."

Eleanor Thorne didn't seem like the type who let things slip her mind.

Bobbie leaned over the desk, speaking quietly. "Is there anyone else here who can tell us about Arrow Springs history?"

"You'll have better luck at the historical society," she said. "They're a little batty about—that is, they're really up on local history."

I turned to Bobbie. "Where's the historical society?"

"It's at Chambers House, over by Strawberry Creek."

"Oh right—by the brewery."

Bobbie chuckled. "Of course, that would be your landmark."

"What? It's a cool brewery. They have, like, 31 different craft beers on tap. Maybe not 31. I'm probably thinking about ice cream, but they have a lot. Can we stop by after?"

"We'll see."

We stepped outside, and I basked in the warm sunshine. "It's not that far. Wanna walk?"

Bobbie headed for the car. "The weather is too unpredictable this time of year and I didn't bring my umbrella."

I squinted in the bright sunlight and counted three fluffy clouds floating by. "Whatever you say."

Five minutes later, we parked in front of the enormous old Chambers House.

I got out of the car. "What style of house is this? It seems sort of Victorian, but kind of plainer."

"They call it Folk Victorian. The people who built it wouldn't have been trying to impress anyone, which is probably why they skipped the gingerbread details."

"That wraparound porch is bigger than the apartment I had in L.A." I led the way up the wooden stairs and pushed open the heavy front door, nearly running right into a woman in a long black dress and a huge hat trimmed in lace and flowers.

"Welcome to Chambers House," she said. "You're just in time for the tour."

I didn't want to spend an hour or longer poking around a dusty old house. "We're not really here for the tour. We wanted to talk to someone about local history and Franklin Norvelt."

"Then you'll want to join the tour." She stepped aside so we could enter an empty foyer area. "Twenty dollars per visitor." She glanced at Bobbie. "Fifteen for seniors."

"Thanks, but we—" I began.

"We'd be delighted to join the tour," Bobbie interrupted. "How lucky we got here in time. Isn't it lucky, Whitley? Let me get out my wallet."

I sighed, and the woman shot a glare at me before smiling and accepting the money Bobbie held out.

"Come in, come in."

The woman in black, who looked a little older than me, introduced her character as Chambers' goddaughter. "When Franklin Norvelt died, his estate was in disarray, and there were questions as to who would inherit his wealth. He held title to two homes, including this one, and several acres of land."

"What about his gold?" I asked.

The woman stiffened and looked down her rather long nose at me. "If you ask questions, I may lose my place and have to start over from the beginning."

"I'm so glad you told us," Bobbie said. "I was about to ask you about your dress. It's quite lovely. And that stunning hat must have been quite fashionable in the... 1890s?"

Apparently questions about fashion were welcome, since the woman and Bobbie had a long discussion about late 19th century styles. Thankfully, they didn't object when I wandered into the next room, a parlor or sitting room.

I passed through into another similar room where a bureau held several photos labeled with names. There was Franklin Norvelt, Mrs. Franklin Norvelt, and a family picture with Mr. and Mrs. and their two sons.

By this time, Bobbie and the tour guide had joined me, and I risked asking another question. "Doesn't Mrs. Norvelt have a first name? I'm guessing it wasn't Franklin like her husband."

Our guide didn't appreciate my attempt at humor. "It was customary to refer to women that way in those days." She turned to Bobbie. "Would you like to tour the bedrooms? They're upstairs."

"Yes, of course," Bobbie said. "I'm a little slow these days, so it may take me longer, but I can make it if you don't mind taking it slowly."

They headed for a carpeted staircase with ornate bannisters that had been polished until they practically glowed.

"I'll be right up." I slipped around the corner, not wanting to spend another minute in Miss Snooty's company. On my right was a velvet rope hung to keep people from going downstairs into the basement, and to the left were two doors. Ahead was what appeared to be an old-fashioned but working kitchen.

A jar of preserves caught my eye, and I wondered if it was a prop. When I picked it up, I found it was full of real preserves that had leaked out, and now I had a sticky mess on my hand.

I hurried to the kitchen sink, but when I turned on the faucet, no water came out. I tried the first door I'd seen, which turned out to be a storage closet with a mop, a shovel, and a vacuum cleaner. The next door turned out to be a bathroom with running water. I washed my hands and dried them on the paper towels provided.

I arrived back at the parlor just as Bobbie and the guide were clomping down the stairs.

"We should probably get going," I said, hoping Bobbie would take the hint.

"Yes, of course. I lost track of the time." She smiled warmly at the woman in black. "You've been very helpful. We'd hoped to talk with Eleanor Thorne at the library. I understand she's something of a local history expert. But you're nearly her match, I would say. How did you learn so much at such a young age?"

The woman beamed. "It's a passion of mine. Our local history is so colorful."

"That's so true." Bobbie pretended not to notice me making faces at her as I stood behind the woman.

"But if you really want to talk to an expert on local history, you should go see Mitsy."

"Mitsy?" I didn't expect that answer. "But she's so young." It was hard to believe someone her age could be an expert on anything.

"Not that Mitsy," the woman said. "Her grandmother."

Triple Shot

After dropping Bobbie off at home, I left the car in the driveway, and Kit and I headed down the hill into town. The sun had dipped behind the mountains, but it would be another hour before sunset.

The sign on Sugar Buns Bakery's door said closed. I tried the door anyway, but it was locked. Peering in, I saw movement. Mitsy was at the back of the room, sweeping. I tapped on the door, and she looked up. She grinned when she noticed me, probably because Kit stood with her front paws on the window, wagging her tail vigorously.

"Well, hello again, sweetie pie." Mitsy crouched down to pet Kit then informed me she'd sold out of cinnamon rolls.

"That's okay. I still have one at home if I get desperate."

"You're so funny, Whit."

"I actually came to ask you about your grandmother. I need some information about Franklin Norvelt, the guy who started Arrow Springs, and I was told she's something of an expert about the early days of the community."

"She is." Mitsy scooped Kit into her arms and stood, rocking the dog like a baby. "She always tells me no one cares about the old days except the people who want to take advantage of her. It's all about money these days. At least that's what Nana says."

"I'd love to hear about the old days." Sure, I had an ulterior motive, but I would never take advantage of an old lady. "Does she still live in town?"

She nodded. "She likes to keep to herself."

"Would you mind calling her and ask if I could stop by and ask her some questions about Norvelt?"

"Why do you want to talk to her?" Mitsy asked, her eyes narrowing ever so slightly.

"It's kind of a long story." I could tell I was about to lose her trust, and I didn't want that to happen. In a rush, I gave her a summary of what I knew so far. "The dead guy who they found in the lake stole a journal that appears to have been written by Franklin Norvelt. I now have that journal, and it might have a clue about where he hid his gold. I'm not after the gold, but I am after the person who attacked me and whoever murdered the book thief. It might be the same person. I'm almost positive the journal, the gold, and the murder are all connected."

Mitsy blinked a few times.

"If there is gold, I want it to go to the right people, not some opportunists who show up in town and take what doesn't belong to them."

Mitsy took in a deep breath and let it out slowly. "I see."

"Did you get all that?" I asked. "Sorry. Sometimes I talk too fast. Bobbie always tells me to slow down."

"I got it." She relocked the front door. "Follow me."

Mitsy led me to the back of the bakery and around a wall. I followed her as she climbed a stairway, still cradling Kit in her arms. At the second floor landing we came upon a heavy door, painted cobalt blue, its brass handle worn smooth. A small wreath of dried lavender hung from a nail.

Mitsy wiped her feet on the welcome mat, then unlocked the door and pushed it open. We entered another world.

Chapter Twenty-One

Had I stepped through one of those inter-dimensional portals Jane had talked about? We stood in a parlor right out of the Victorian era, with dark green flocked wallpaper, antique furniture, and Persian rugs covering nearly every inch of the floor.

I'd been in movie sets that felt like stepping back in time, but there was always something that ruined the effect. If the fake-old furniture didn't do it, the set lights and boom mikes did.

"This place is amazing," I said, my voice barely above a whisper.

"Thanks." Mitsy smiled proudly. "We like it. Have a seat, and I'll get my grandma."

Everything looked too old and fragile to sit on, so I stayed on my feet, walking around the room admiring the antiques. Against one wall, a bookcase nearly overflowed with books, most old, but one shelf held newer books, mostly bestsellers. One of Marty's memoirs was wedged in the middle.

Mitsy reappeared without my dog. "My grandmother is comfy in her room, so she said it was okay to bring you in."

"She and Kit are comfy?" That dog was such a charmer. Maybe I could learn a thing or two from her.

"I've been telling her about Kit for weeks and weeks." Mitsy grinned. "She hardly ever lets people come visit, but we both agreed that anyone with a dog like Kit must be okay."

I wanted to tell her not to be so naïve, but I held my tongue.

We walked past a small kitchen that had been modernized with new appliances including a dishwasher. A short hallway led to her grandmother's bedroom.

The elder Mitsy sat with her feet up in a recliner beside a four-poster bed draped with several beautifully sewn quilts. She wore a deep purple velour robe with Kit happily curled up in her lap. Her white hair was a halo of curls hovering over a wrinkled face with rouged cheeks and a proud chin.

What caught my attention was her bright blue eyes that sparkled with vitality rarely seen in people half her age.

Mitsy introduced me. "This is Whitley Leland."

"Welcome, my dear." Her voice was surprisingly strong and vibrant. "Come sit down here next to me. Mimi has told me so much about you, although to be honest, she talked about your dog much more than you. Would you like a cup of tea?"

I took a seat in the wingback chair she motioned to. "No, thank you. I'm fine."

Mitsy stayed standing. "I'll put the kettle on. We always have tea together after I close up the bakery. Are you sure you wouldn't like a cup?"

"Well, if it's no bother." I felt like a character in a period play, doing my best to remember my lines.

The old woman got right to the point. "Now, what did you want to see me about?"

"Did you hear about Daniel Holland, the thief who they fished out of the lake?"

"Yes, of course. Mimi keeps me up to date on all the important news. I can't help but wonder if he's the sort of man anyone would miss. Even a criminal deserves to be mourned, don't you think?"

I gave her a halfhearted shrug. "I noticed you call your granddaughter Mimi."

"When she was little, it was confusing having the two of us with the same name. Later, in her early teens, as I recall, she didn't care for being called Mitsy. Too old-fashioned, I suppose. And she got teased for it, though she never said anything."

"Kids can be cruel. With a name like Whitley, I got called witless, Whit the Twit, all kinds of things. But when I started taking karate classes, they stopped taunting me." They stopped talking to me altogether, but she didn't need to know that.

She fixed me with a firm gaze. "Daniel Holland was murdered. Isn't that true?"

"That's right."

"And your grandmother works with Bernard Fernsby and Arrow Investigations."

"Yes." I was impressed by how much she knew about what went on in our little town.

"And you're helping investigate the murder?" Her bright blue eyes held my gaze. "Why?"

"It's kind of personal." I wasn't sure how much I needed to tell her without overwhelming her with my theories. "I was injected with a powerful sedative, locked in a basement room, and left to die." I didn't know that for sure, but it seemed likely. "I'm almost positive the person who did that to me is the same one who killed Daniel Holland, or it was an accomplice of theirs."

As I spoke, anger flashed across her face for a moment before her expression returned to its previous calm composure. "And you think I can help you in some way?" Age might have slowed her physically, but her mind seemed as quick as ever.

"Daniel Holland stole a book from the basement of Birch Street Books."

Mitsy returned with a tea tray, which she set on a nearby table. She poured two cups, handing one to her grandmother before passing me the other.

"Milk or sugar?" she asked.

"I take it straight, thanks."

"I'll let you two talk." Mitsy leaned over to give her grandmother a kiss on the cheek. "I'll be in the kitchen if you need me," she said and left the room.

The old woman took a sip of her tea, the cup shaking slightly in her hand. "Tell me about this book. You think it's important in some way, don't you?"

I nodded. "It appears to be a journal written by Franklin Norvelt, the founder of Arrow Springs. It's in code."

"Ah, that's not surprising, considering what my grandmother told me about him."

That got my attention. "Your grandmother knew Norvelt?"

"Intimately." She smiled mischievously. "Franklin Norvelt was my grandfather."

She must have noticed my surprise, even though I tried to hide it. I was chatting with a direct descendent of the town's founder. That meant the Mitsy who supplied me with cinnamon rolls was Franklin Norvelt's great-great-granddaughter.

The elder Mitsy leaned forward in her chair. "You think this journal might help you solve the murder?"

"I do. You see, there's a so-called society—a group of people who claim to be looking for some sort of portal."

She gave me a quizzical look. "A portal? To where?"

"Jane Jones, who owns Birch Street Books, claims it might lead to another dimension or another time, but I'm pretty sure it's a scam. My theory is that Jane is using the others to help her find what she's really looking for."

"And what is that?"

"The gold Norvelt hid somewhere before he died."

The elder Mitsy chuckled, and I waited to hear what was so funny.

"That's why Jane decided to buy that old bookshop."

"Exactly. Because it was once Norvelt's house," I said.

"Except Franklin Norvelt didn't live there. Not really. It was his wife's house, and from what my grand-

163

mother told me, Norvelt spent as little time there as possible."

"They didn't live together?" I asked, trying to keep up.

"I see I've confused you. My grandmother was Norvelt's mistress. She would have been his second wife, but Mrs. Norvelt refused to give him a divorce. She liked the position she held in society as the founder's wife."

All this history was interesting if you liked that sort of thing, but I struggled to focus as she talked. If there was gold hidden in town, I wanted to find it before Jane did. As descendants of Norvelt, Mitsy and her grandmother might be the rightful heirs to his fortune.

When there was a break in her story, I asked, "Can I read you the part of the journal that I decoded?"

"Please do."

"This is from one of the last pages of the journal," I explained before reading from my notes. "I have entrusted the location of my remaining wealth to my most trusted confidant." I paused and waited for a reaction. "Do you have any idea who that most trusted confidant might be?"

"It could be several people. Is there more after that?"

I didn't see how the next part would help, but I read it anyway. "...knowing that when the time is right, destiny will guide its discovery into the hands of those who will use its riches for the betterment of all."

A grin spread across the elder Mitsy's face. "Destiny," she said, her voice strong and vibrant. "That was my grandmother's name."

Chapter Twenty-Two

I gasped, then reread the passage, now knowing that Destiny had been a person.

"Destiny will guide its discovery into the hands of those who will use its riches for the betterment of all." As I spoke, the old woman's grin only broadened. "Your grandmother knew where the gold was hidden?"

"The treasure was the land, the homes, and the farms. Norvelt put all the deeds in Destiny's name, knowing that she would do the right thing. And she did. After Norvelt died, everyone who'd been a part of the community—man, woman, and child—was given a plot of land. If they'd built a house, she made sure they owned the land it stood on. She did her best to divvy up the land fairly, but I'm sure you won't be surprised to learn that certain people didn't like some of her decisions. Norvelt's wife was the loudest and angriest of all of them. Not surprising, really, since she accused Destiny of stealing her husband. The community became divided between those who supported Norvelt's wife and those who supported Destiny."

"What did she do about that?" I asked, now hanging on every word.

"Destiny met with each of the dissenters and offered them twice what their land was worth if they left and never came back. Most took her up on the offer. After that, Norvelt's wife didn't have much support. She went to Destiny and demanded four times what her home and land were worth. She threatened to burn everything down if she didn't get it. Destiny didn't think she had much choice, so she bought her out."

"What a..." I stopped myself from saying what I wanted to. "What an awful person. I hate to think she got away with threatening her like that."

Mitsy's grandmother took another sip of tea. "After Destiny and the others incorporated as Arrow Springs, the land values skyrocketed. And Norvelt's wife died a bitter, lonely old woman. At least that's the way my grandmother told the story."

I picked up my teacup and sipped the lukewarm liquid while I thought about what I'd learned. It was hard to believe that the town's history had something to do with Daniel Holland's murder and my attack, but I sensed they were very important.

"Where did Norvelt and Destiny live?"

"We're sitting in the second floor of Destiny's home right now. The downstairs was once the living areas and kitchen, but when she passed away, my husband and I turned the downstairs into a bakery."

She seemed lost in a memory, and I waited for her to continue.

Her eyes fluttered as she returned to the present. "Norvelt never spent the night here. He was afraid his wife would show up and cause problems, and he was probably right. Norvelt had a house built on the outskirts of town for himself and Destiny. As far as anyone knew, it belonged to his closest friend and ally, Samuel Chambers, but Chambers lived in a smaller house on the property."

Something about that name rang a bell. "Oh! The Chambers House."

"That's the place. Chambers died childless, so he left his home and everything else to the town. It took many years to have it designated a historic monument."

"We just went on a tour." Or rather, I hung around while Bobbie toured. "The furniture and wallpaper and stuff seemed really authentic."

"It's been kept exactly the way it was when Chambers passed away."

"You know, I was never into history," I admitted. "But hearing you talk about it really brings the past to life. Still..." I hesitated. "I'm kinda disappointed there's no hidden treasure."

"A childish wish, isn't it?" she said as her granddaughter reentered the room. "But real treasure is so much easier to find. It's all around us in this miraculous world. All you have to do is open your heart."

"And your eyes," the younger Mitsy said with a wink.

After taking a sleeping Kit from her grandmother's arms, Mitsy showed me down the stairs and unlocked the front door. She set Kit on the floor, and after the dog gave a shake, I clipped her leash onto her harness.

"Please don't tell anyone my grandmother lives upstairs. I'm worried about her safety, especially with what you told us today. It seems like someone is willing to murder to get their hands on this treasure, whether it exists or not. If they think my grandmother knows something that will lead them to it—"

"I won't tell a soul. You have my promise."

She let out a sigh, then surprised me with a hug. "Thank you, Whit. You're a good friend." She held the door open for me.

I stepped onto the sidewalk and led Kit to the nearest patch of grass as I thought about what Mitsy had said. She'd called me a friend. I'd first met Mitsy a few months ago, and I wondered when I'd gone from customer to friend.

There were bigger things to think about at the moment, but I felt a bit lighter knowing I'd somehow made a friend.

When I arrived home, Bobbie already had her coat on and her purse over her shoulder.

"Going somewhere?" I asked.

"Bernard is ready to brief us on the background checks he performed. This should be interesting." She opened the door and stepped outside, stopping only to call over her shoulder, "Are you coming?"

I looked at Kit. "I guess we don't get to sit on the sofa and snuggle after all."

Bobbie held Kit on her lap as I drove us to Arrow Investigations, and I told Bobbie about having tea with Mitsy's grandmother. "She says the wealth Franklin Norvelt wrote about was the land, the farms, and the homes. I wonder if she's right."

"It would explain why no one's ever found a pot of gold."

Once we were settled in Bernard's office, Kit fell asleep again in Bobbie's lap. I repeated my conversation with Mitsy, Franklin Norvelt's granddaughter. Bernard was surprised to hear she was still alive.

"I met her years ago, and she seemed quite old then." He chuckled. "She was probably younger than I am now. Would you like to hear the results of my background checks?"

"I can hardly wait." I even sort of meant it.

Several manila folders were piled on his desk. Opening the first one, Jane Jones' file, he began to summarize, though he gave more details than I thought was necessary.

According to Bernard and his sources, not only was Jane Jones two or three years too old to have been Kelvin's third grade classmate, Marnie, she'd grown up in New Jersey, hundreds of miles from Kelvin.

I always found it hard to sit still and listen, something often noted on my report cards, so I stood. "Stretching my legs" was as good an excuse as any. I half listened as I perused the books on the shelf. Mostly textbooks. I pulled out a book titled *A General Theory of Crime* and flipped through it.

"And that's everything on Ms. Jane Jones." Bernard closed the folder and moved on to the next.

I returned the book to its place. "It's very neat and orderly, isn't it?"

"I do my best to stay organized," Bernard said as he opened another file. "Next up, Victor Zhang."

"I meant Jane's life has been neat and orderly. Whose life is that regimented? And I don't buy her working for that corporation right out of college, then quitting to open a bookstore."

"Some people's lives have a more direct trajectory than others," Bobbie said. "And after what you've told us, the corporation was surely a cover for the C.I.A. or other intelligence organization. They probably recruited her right out of college."

Bernard cleared his throat. "May I proceed with the next file now?"

Bobbie answered for both of us. "Yes, of course. Perhaps just the highlights?"

The highlights took another twenty minutes, and the only important information I got from it was that Leo's alibi checked out. Arrow Pharmacy was small, staffed by only one pharmacist, one pharmacy tech, and one clerk. According to Bernard, the pharmacy tech swore that Leo was there the entire day from before they opened at nine until six that evening, except for a thirty- to forty-five minute lunch break. "The timing of his break lines up with when the others said he was at Purrs and Pours with them."

"Hold on," I interrupted. "Leo is the only one of the group who wasn't at Purrs and Pours at around noon when I was attacked. And he has access to drugs like pronapol—"

"Propofol," Bobbie corrected. "What are you suggesting? That the technician is lying?"

"That's exactly what I'm suggesting. Maybe Leo got the tech to lie for him."

Bernard nodded. "I'll see what I can do to poke holes in the tech's story." He moved Leo's file aside and opened the next. "Now on to Eleanor Thorne."

I rubbed my hands together. "This should be good." I had high hopes for some interesting tidbits about Eleanor. No one could be that strait-laced all the time. After hearing about her upbringing, years of education, and extensive travel, I began to change my opinion.

My stomach growled. "Anyone ready for tacos?"

Bobbie gave me an amused look. "Are you that bored?"

"The tacos at the taco joint downstairs are really good. I started thinking about them as soon as you told me we were coming to Bernard's office."

Bobbie pulled a couple of bills out of her purse and handed them to me. "Get me the usual and whatever you and Bernard want. I'll fill you in on any important details you miss."

By the time I returned with the tacos, they'd moved on to Nora Nettle's file. We took a break to avoid spilling guacamole over any of the papers. After we finished eating, Bobbie gave me one of her sweetest smiles. That meant she was going to ask me to do something I probably didn't want to do.

"Why don't you make copies of the contents of the files we've gone over so far?"

"I thought we weren't keeping physical copies."

"That only pertained to anything confidential Jane told us," Bernard said. "Everything in these files is in the public records."

"Fine." I figured it gave me something to do while Bernard droned on for another hour.

After returning Eleanor Thorne's report to her file, I took the stack of copies back to the office, and Bernard handed me Mrs. Nettle's file.

"We're on the last one," Bobbie said. "Martin Blackwood."

"Oh." It hadn't occurred to me that they'd investigate him, but of course it made sense. "I think I'll sit and listen in."

Marty's story had as many boring details as the others until he became a war correspondent at the age of twenty-four. He spent much of the next six years in Afghanistan, spending a month or two at his parents' vacation home in Arrow Springs before returning to the front lines.

I perked up when Bernard said, "He never married, though he was engaged."

"Yeah, she died."

Bernard looked up from the papers. "What made you say that?"

"Oh, sorry. Just a wild guess. Was I wrong?"

Bernard stared at me for a moment, then shook his head. "Not every relationship ends in death or murder, Whitley. Sometimes people just drift apart. Maybe spending so much time out of the country put a strain on the relationship."

"Or maybe he wasn't in love with her. Or maybe—"

"If you're that curious," Bobbie interrupted, "you could always ask him."

"Yeah, no. I'd rather come up with increasingly wild theories about why he's single. It's way more fun and less likely to piss him off. I kind of like having a few friends in town."

"A few?" Bobbie raised her eyebrows as if she doubted me.

"At least two." Was Kelvin a friend? What about Elijah? "Maybe three or four."

"Whitley Leland." Bobbie's voice held a note of pride. "You never cease to surprise me."

Chapter Twenty-Three

Bernard closed Marty's file and set it on top of the others.

"Why do you think Marty got involved with the Society?" It didn't make sense to me.

"Is this another question you can't ask Marty?" Bobbie patted my arm. "If he really is a friend, you should be able to ask him anything."

Was that true? Was I willing to risk it?

"Yeah, you're right. Besides, it's going to bug me until I know what he's up to. If he's involved somehow with the person who murdered Daniel and attacked me, I'd rather know now."

"Or persons." Bernard leaned forward on his desk. "It could be two different people, or more than two for that matter."

"Do you think it's some sort of plot?" Bobbie tapped her chin. "The entire society might be in on it together for all we know. Their alibis mean nothing if they all agreed to cover for each other."

I hated the idea that Marty was one of the people Bobbie was suggesting was part of some conspiracy. "This is getting way too complicated." I pulled my phone from my pocket and sent Marty a text asking to meet up. "Want a ride home?" I asked Bobbie who wasn't showing any signs of leaving.

"I think I'll stay here a bit longer so Bernard and I can do some brainstorming."

My phone buzzed with a reply from Marty. *I can meet now.*

I answered: *Where?*

I looked up to see Bobbie and Bernard watching me expectantly. "He wants me to come to his place."

"No." Bobbie's tone became deadly serious. "Absolutely not. You will not meet anyone alone until this case is solved, do you understand?"

"Well, that's not going to work unless you plan to follow me everywhere."

Bobbie began digging through her purse. She kept an endless supply of cough drops, tissues, aspirin and any other item that might be needed in a minor emergency. I couldn't see how any of those were going to help at that moment.

"Voila!" She brandished a small blister pack with what looked like one of my grandfather's old hearing aid batteries which she held out to me. "Do you know how to set one of these up?"

I took it and read the label. It appeared identical to the eavesdropping devices Kelvin had shown us. "No. Absolutely not. I'm not going to have you listening to my entire conversation with Marty. What if he found out I had it?"

Bobbie frowned and put the package back in her purse.

I wasn't about to let her pouting get me to change my mind. "How about this? I'll text you when I arrive and when I leave. If I haven't left in thirty minutes, I'll give you an update. If at any time you don't hear from me, you have permission to come to my rescue."

"I don't like it," she said. "Why can't you meet somewhere like Purrs and Pours?"

"With Mrs. Nettle eavesdropping on our conversation? No way. Besides, I think I'm allergic to cats. Or maybe Mrs. N." I grinned. "Bobbie, I'll be fine. I promise."

"Maybe I should go along and wait in the car."

"You'll get more done if you stay here and help Bernard." I didn't really think Bernard needed her help, but I didn't want to explain to Marty why my grandmother was waiting for me in the car outside his house.

"She'll be fine, Bobbie," Bernard said, coming to my defense.

"Then take Kit with you," Bobbie suggested.

"Really?" As if a six-pound dog would protect me. "She's kind of a distraction. Can't she stay with you?"

"Fine." Bobbie sighed loudly then dug into her purse and handed me a small, square plastic item. "At least take this tracker with you. Just in case."

"Fine," I mumbled, shoving it into my pocket. My grandmother sure loved her gadgets.

Marty gave me directions to his house on the outskirts of town. I drove along a winding road that climbed higher with each curve. He'd told me to look for a steep driveway which I was to turn into and park at the top.

What he called steep seemed nearly vertical, and I held my breath until I reached the top. The house appeared modest from the front—a typical mountain cabin with redwood siding and stone chimney.

Marty came down the front steps to meet me as I got out of my car. He wore a cashmere V-neck sweater, looking even more ruggedly handsome than when we'd first met. I bit my lip and asked myself what I was getting into.

"What do you do when the roads get icy?" I asked.

"I'm practically a hermit, remember? Winter gives me an excuse to stay indoors for months at a time."

"How do you get food?"

"I have it airdropped."

"You're joking right?"

He grinned. "Yes, but I'm looking forward to the day when drones can drop my groceries by my front door."

"I bet Kelvin could hook you up. He's got some awesome drones. One of them kinda saved my life one time."

His eyes widened. "Now you're joking."

I laughed. "No, I'm really not. I'll have to tell you all about it sometime. Right now," I pulled out my phone. "I have to text Bobbie." After I sent the text, I set the timer for thirty minutes so I wouldn't forget.

"Does she always keep tabs on you like that?"

"Only when there's a murderer running around loose,

which seems to happen around here more often that you might expect."

Marty invited me to come inside. The sparsely furnished interior was simple with white walls and wood floors. A comfy sofa and chairs faced an empty fireplace.

"Nice place." There was one extravagance. The shelves overflowed with books.

"I don't entertain much," he said. "Or at all, really. I spent the last twenty minutes throwing everything in closets."

I rubbed my arms wishing I'd worn something warmer than a thin sweatshirt.

"C'mon. It's much warmer in the kitchen. I hate heating the whole house, so I spend most of my time in there."

I passed a bookshelf with several framed photos. Marty caught me staring at a picture of a dark-haired young woman.

"That's Rebecca."

"Your fiancé?"

He tilted his head and staredt at me for several seconds before answering. "I suppose I should have expected you'd do a background check on me."

"Bernard did one on all the society members."

"I'm just... not used to people knowing things about me that I haven't told them. I was briefly engaged to a woman I'd been dating for a couple of years. We had a great relationship as long as we didn't spend too much time together. I'm not even sure which one of us broke it off. After living together for a few months, we both knew it wasn't going to work." He picked up the picture I'd been eyeing. "Rebecca was a soldier in Afghanistan. I'd never felt like that about anyone until her."

"She's the one who died in your arms?"

He set the frame down and turned to me. "Coffee?"

I followed Marty through a swinging door into the kitchen. He was right—it was much warmer. A desk with two large monitors was squeezed in the corner leaving just enough room for a small kitchen table and one chair.

Marty swung his desk chair over to the table and invited me to sit. He poured the coffee, offered cream and sugar, then took his seat across from me.

"What do you want to know?" he asked.

"Direct and to the point," I said. "I like that."

"Darn. It usually throws people off. I'm starting to think you're not like other people."

"You're not the first person who's told me that." I never knew if it was meant as a compliment or an insult. "I'd really like to know how you got involved with the Society for Ancient Wisdom. You don't seem to have much in common with any of them."

"Can what I tell you be confidential?" he asked.

"Sure. As long as it's not connected to anything illegal." I thought about what I'd just said. "Actually, I don't care if it's illegal as long as it's not connected to the murder or me being attacked." I considered again, and added, "And as long as it's not hurting anyone."

"I'm not sure what's left, but okay." He stirred his coffee as he seemed to be deciding where to begin. "I went to journalism school, planning to have a career as an investigative journalist. Turns out, like most things, you have to work your way up, pay your dues, and all that. It meant either grunt work at a major newspaper or working for a small local paper covering town council meetings and high school football games. I was impatient, so when the opportunity to cover the war in Afghanistan came along, I jumped at it." He paused. "It changed me."

"I can imagine it did." I didn't know what this had to do with Jane and the others, but I let him continue.

"I wrote the first book mostly for myself so I wouldn't forget what I'd learned about right and wrong, how I'd grown as a human being and how the war had changed me. The first book was all about me, but after it was published, I realized how privileged I'd been to be that close to war but not involved. I watched young kids face hardships like nothing I'd ever experienced. I watched them risk their lives through a camera lens."

"So, you wrote another book?"

He nodded. "I saw firsthand what a teenage kid could do when they had to. It was inspiring at first. But after a year or two, I couldn't shake the feeling that they shouldn't have to be so resourceful. They shouldn't have to fight our battles."

"And both books were best sellers."

"After that, I didn't know what to do next. I wasn't sure I deserved the success and I sure as hell didn't think I could repeat it. I came to Arrow Springs to get away from everything for a while. I stopped thinking about the world, and evil, and everything that was going on 'out there.'" He waved his hands vaguely, but I knew what he meant. "Arrow Springs didn't feel like the real world. That's what I liked about it. Not long after I moved back permanently, I took a tour of Chambers House."

"Bobbie and I just went there. It was my first time."

"Pretty cheesy, right? I got the feeling they'd completely whitewashed the history of the colony and the town, so I started doing my own research. That's how I met Eleanor Thorne. She's the closest we have to a town historian."

It all started to fall into place. "And Eleanor introduced you to the others?"

He nodded. "I thought they were all a bit nutty at first with all the talk about portals and doors to other dimensions, but I played along. It started as a distraction, and I suppose I was hungry for companionship. I'd gotten into the habit of avoiding people. I hated all the questions about the war. I wanted to forget all about it."

"Yeah, I get it. I feel that way when people ask me about my gymnastics career, and I didn't have to watch anyone die. Well, except my mother's hopes and dreams. She had her heart set on having an Olympic medalist in the family."

"If it makes you feel any better, my parents don't understand my choices either. I used their vacation cabin —this cabin—between assignments, and since I came back for good, they've left me alone pretty much." He shrugged. "I don't usually talk about myself this much. There's something you should know about Jane. Ready?"

"Ready."

"We both know she's not looking for a portal to another world." He leaned forward, and in a hushed voice, he said, "She's looking for gold."

"Uh-huh. And?"

"You already knew? But how? Did Jane tell you?"

The surprised look on his face made me laugh despite myself. "No, I figured it out with a little help from my friends."

He frowned. "I was feeling pretty smart until now."

I shrugged one shoulder. "Maybe we're both smart. Who else is in on the treasure hunt? All of them?"

"I figured it was just Jane. Do you know something I don't?"

"Only that Eleanor lied, and Leo has drugs, and he probably knows how to use a syringe."

"Good points. What about Mrs. Nettle?"

"Really? Mrs. 'I can talk to cats and also raccoons'? That Mrs. Nettle?"

"I see what you mean."

My phone buzzed. "Gotta check in." I sent a text to Bobbie then carried my coffee cup to the sink the way Bobbie had trained me. "Thanks for the coffee and the information."

Marty walked me to the door. "Thanks for listening." He took my hand and gave it a squeeze.

"Anything else you haven't told me?" I asked, wondering if he'd left out any important information.

"Yeah." He leaned against the door, still holding my hand. "I like you, Whitley."

"Um..." I felt awkward, not sure what to say. "I like you, too."

He smiled and took a step closer. "It's been a long time since I felt close to anyone." He was close enough for me to see flecks of gold in his brown irises.

"And I'd really like to kiss you, but, well... things have

changed since I last dated anyone. Am I supposed to ask first?"

I don't know why that seemed so funny—maybe it was the tension—but I broke into laughter. "Sorry, sorry."

It must have taken me a minute to compose myself, and then I kissed him. Then he kissed me. It was a whole kissy thing that went on for a while until I knew I'd better slow things down and take a step back.

I literally took a step back and said, "If you turn out to have anything to do with Daniel's murder, I will murder you myself."

Chapter Twenty-Four

I'd just turned my car around, preparing to head back down the steep driveway, when I got a text from Bobbie asking me to meet her at Jane's bookshop.

"Good for her," I muttered to myself. "She's finally getting the hang of texting."

As I drove, I wondered who we were meeting and why she'd gone there by herself, when she'd warned me about meeting anyone alone. But since Bobbie didn't drive, someone must have gone with her. Maybe Bernard or Rosa. Rosa would be thrilled to be involved and would no doubt have a purse weighed down with at least three or four weapons.

The street in front of the shop had temporary "no parking" signs posted, so I pulled around the corner and found a spot on a side street. As I approached the front door, I waved at Kelvin in case he was watching through his binoculars. I even waved at Herman as he washed and squeegeed the front windows but only got a glare in return.

I entered the bookshop, which seemed eerily quiet. How Jane managed to make a profit when they got so few customers, I had no idea. Maybe that's why she needed to find a pot of gold.

"Jane?" I called out. "Bobbie?"

I took a second look at Bobbie's text. She'd sent it only ten minutes earlier, so maybe she was on her way. A little voice told me to wait out front, but I didn't want them starting without me. Starting what, I didn't know, but I hated to think I might miss out on some important information.

As I made my way to the back of the bookshop, the little voice in my head grew louder. As I was about to turn around and leave, a faint voice called my name.

It came from the direction of the basement door, which stood slightly ajar. I approached slowly, wondering what I was getting myself into.

Then I heard Bobbie's voice. "Whit? Is that you?"

"Thank goodness." I pulled the door open and headed down the steps. "What are you doing in the basement?"

A woman's voice called back. "I'm showing your grandmother where I think the portal is located."

I froze halfway down the steps. "Bobbie? Is everything okay?"

"Whit?" Bobbie's voice sounded fainter.

I crept down the stairs, doing my best not to make a sound, even though I'd already lost the element of surprise. I had no idea what Jane was up to, but I knew I could take her. As long as she didn't have a gun.

But what if she did? What if Jane killed Daniel and now planned to kill Bobbie and me because we'd gotten too close to the truth?

The smart thing to do would be to get the heck out of the bookshop and call the police. But what if Bobbie was in immediate danger? What if something happened to her because I'd played it safe for once in my life?

I ducked behind one of the bookshelves and peered through the spaces between the books, but I didn't see anyone. I made my way to the end of the aisle and turned the corner, but the room seemed empty.

A touch on my arm made me jump out of my skin. I spun around to find Mrs. Nettle in an oversized t-shirt that read, "Just Kitten Around."

"Shhh…" she said. "Jane's in the other room with your grandmother."

"What are they doing?" I hoped she'd say they were sharing a nice pot of tea.

"I think Jane's gone over the edge," she whispered. "She's searching for gold. Can you imagine? We're on the brink of a discovery unlike anything the world has seen in decades, and she's focused on material wealth. Maybe you can talk to her."

"Does she have a gun?" I asked, just to be on the safe side.

Her eyes widened. "I don't think so. Do you think she does? Should we go get help? I'm sure she won't hurt your grandmother. At least I hope she won't."

What an annoying woman! "Where are they?"

Mrs. Nettle gestured for me to follow her to an open door. There seemed to be an endless number of rooms in this basement. I rushed through the door, hoping to surprise Jane, but all I found was an empty room.

"Bobbie?" I whispered, but no one answered.

I was about to ask Mrs. Nettle what was going on when I noticed the open trapdoor in the floor. Before I could react, she gave me a hard shove.

I landed hard on a dirt floor, but luckily, I'd had lots of practice falling without injuring myself. My arm was going to be sore for a while, though.

In the dim light, I got to my feet and took in my surroundings. It seemed to be a sub-basement, with unfinished walls and ancient, rusty pipes running overhead.

As my eyes adjusted, I saw I wasn't alone. "Jane?"

Jane sat on the ground, dirt sticking to her sweaty face. She didn't look any happier seeing me than I did seeing her. "I was kind of hoping you'd come rescue me, but I guess the old bat is smarter than both of us."

Getting to my feet, I asked, "Where's Bobbie?"

Jane pointed up at Mrs. Nettle, who peered down from at least eight feet above us. She held her phone up and Bobbie's voice called to me. "Whit? Is that you?"

She'd recorded or maybe cloned Bobbie's voice. Clever. "And what about the text?" I asked. "Did you send that too?"

Mrs. Nettle's smug smile made me want to punch her, but that would have to wait. "It's not hard at all to send a text that looks like it came from another number. I guess that's something your grandmother forgot to teach you."

"What are you planning to do with us?" My voice sounded more confident than I felt.

She answered by throwing down a shovel. I glanced at Jane, who held up her own.

"Break's over. Get back to work." She sneered at us and slammed the trapdoor shut.

The only light came from a small electric lantern and what little filtered through the narrow gaps in the wooden trapdoor. The boards were rough and slightly warped from the dampness surrounding me.

Standing on my tiptoes, I reached for the ceiling, but it was a good foot higher than my reach. When I was a gymnast, I could jump sixteen inches straight up, which was better than most of the shorter girls, but otherwise not that impressive.

I took a few steps back, then ran and leaped into the air, grabbing for the trapdoor frame. My fingertips hit the edge, giving me a tiny hope.

"What are you doing?" Jane asked, scowling at me. "If she hears you..." Her voice trailed off.

"I'm trying to get out of here," I hissed. More of a running start would help. I did my best to remember how far back to jump to get the most height and traced a line in the dirt.

Ignoring Jane's glare, I paced the steps all the way to the wall, which gave me about four feet to gain momentum. After a few deep breaths, I took off. Step, step, step, jump. My hand hit the trapdoor, but I didn't come close to being able to grab hold.

Jane had picked up her shovel and started digging as best as she could, sitting on the ground.

"You're helping her?" I asked, dumbfounded.

She shot me a glare. "You'd better help too if you want to stay alive."

"She's threatened to kill you?" I couldn't believe my ears. "We're talking about Mrs. Nettle?"

"If I want food or water, I have to dig." She pressed her lips together in an angry grimace. "I defended the old bat when people made fun of her, calling her a crazy cat lady. She's crazy like a fox. She threw me down here yesterday afternoon and told me to dig. I went all night and most of the day without food or water before I decided I wasn't ready to die. You can't live long without water, you know."

I examined the hole she'd managed to dig. A couple of feet wide and maybe a foot deep, if that. "You haven't made much progress."

"Thanks for noticing," she said, the sarcasm in her voice impossible to miss. "It's not like I haven't heard her screaming at me telling me the same thing. It's not easy when you can't stand."

I reached into my pocket and pulled out all the contents. Phone with no signal. Lip balm. Car key. The tracker Bobbie had given me. For a brief moment, hope swelled inside me before I remembered we were under the basement. No way would the signal reach Bobbie.

Frustrated, I threw them on the ground. I walked the perimeter of the small space looking for any opening or door, but all I found was something resembling an industrial vacuum cleaner and an old boiler, rusted and covered in dust and spider webs. The thought of spiders made me shiver.

Jane watched me. "The only way out is the way we came in. Up there." She pointed to the hole I'd been shoved through. "This crawl space was boarded up when the owner put in a new heating and AC system."

"Are you sure?" I began tapping along the walls, listening for a hollow sound.

"Quiet," Jane hissed. "If she hears you..." She didn't finish the sentence, but considering Mrs. N. had already trapped me in a crawl space, I didn't see how much more she could do to me.

The trapdoor thudded open. "Are you digging?" Mrs. Nettle's syrupy voice made my skin crawl. Her round face appeared over the side of the opening above, her eyes flashing in the dim light.

"Just getting settled in, checking out my new digs," I said flippantly.

Her eyes narrowed. "You think this is funny? Maybe you'd like to know what I had delivered earlier today."

She waited for my response, but I wasn't taking the bait.

Clapping her hands in glee, she cried out, "A rattlesnake! Would you like a pet to keep you company, Whitley? Perhaps it would help motivate you."

I clenched my fists, frustration tightening all my muscles. "No need. I'm more than happy to dig you a hole." I grabbed my shovel and stabbed the ground with it.

"I'm happy to hear that. I'll be back shortly, and I'll look forward to seeing your progress." The hatch shut, and we were again left in near darkness.

Despite the chilly air, I began to sweat. Jane leaned on one elbow, struggling to use her shovel like a garden trowel.

"Why don't you rest for a while?" I could dig enough

dirt for both of us. "While I'm digging, you can bring me up to speed."

She let her shovel fall to the ground as she collapsed on her side, breathing heavily.

"First question, am I digging for gold?"

"Yes," she said, as if that's all she had strength to say.

I tossed the dirt onto the growing pile. "How'd you figure out where the gold was hidden?"

"Franklin Norvelt lived here." Jane spoke quietly, and I did the same, not wanting Mrs. Nettle to hear us.

I stopped digging long enough to correct her. "His wife lived here, you mean."

"Yes, he and his wife lived here with their sons," she huffed.

Smiling inwardly, I returned to digging. Jane could be as huffy as she wanted, but she didn't know about the other woman in Norvelt's life. Maybe I'd tell her later when I shared the many ways her scheme went wrong. For now, I encouraged her to continue talking.

"I'd found a number of old journals, including the one Daniel stole." She paused, but when she continued, her voice was stronger. "Eleanor had already decoded it. It told us there was a treasure, but it didn't give us any clues about where it was hidden."

That explained why she'd left it out in the open.

"I panicked a bit when you told me someone had stolen a book," she continued. "I'd just come across another journal written by a woman calling herself Destiny."

"Destiny?" I didn't want to give away what I knew, so I said, "Interesting name."

"It was obviously his wife writing under an alias. When we decoded her journal, it told us the gold was buried under her house."

"Daniel must have overheard you and Eleanor talking about the journals and the treasure."

"How could he have heard us?"

"The cats. Daniel had put eavesdropping devices on their collars."

Her jaw dropped. "Those were Daniel's cats that kept getting into the shop?"

"Mrs. Nettle's cats, actually. Daniel stole them to spy on you."

"How did he manage that?" She asked, but I wanted my questions answered first.

"When you learned the gold was buried under the bookshop, how did you figure out it was right here?" I gestured at the hole that was now at least two feet deep.

"Eleanor and I scanned the entire foundation with a metal detector several times, but it never showed anything. She told me she wasn't going to help me anymore. She called it a fool's mission," she grumbled.

"But you didn't give up."

She shook her head. "I got an industrial, high-power unit that can detect metal five feet under the surface."

"Oh." The thing I'd thought was a vacuum cleaner was her metal detector. "How'd you get that thing down here? You must have had someone to help you." I had a feeling I knew who she chose as her new partner.

She sheepishly stared at the ground. "I figured since Eleanor had given up on finding the gold, I could get someone else to help me and keep a bigger share of the treasure."

"Mrs. Nettle."

"I gave her five hundred dollars and promised her ten percent of whatever we found if she kept it a secret from the others. All she seemed to care about was keeping her cat café going, and that would have been a lot of money for her."

I dug for a few minutes in silence before I asked the question I most wanted answered. "Who killed Daniel?"

"I don't know."

"Baloney." I leaned on the shovel and waited to hear whatever story she'd come up with.

"I really don't know." She stared at the ground. "I came down to the basement and found him. I knew Daniel, and I knew it wouldn't look good if he was found dead in my basement."

"You knew him? How?" I asked. "Was he a spy, too?"

"I wasn't a spy." She shook her head in frustration. "But Daniel was. And a traitor. I was sent on a simple mission—an errand really. They needed a nobody to deliver an envelope to Daniel and retrieve a package from him. The only problem was, he picked that day to fake his own death."

"What happened?"

"When I got there, I saw smoke, and like a fool, I ran in to make sure no one was inside. I made it to the kitchen before the explosion. I don't remember anything after that until I ended up in the hospital."

"Is that why you're in a wheelchair?" When she nodded, I said, "No wonder you killed him."

Her voice rose. "I didn't kill him." Then in a hushed voice, she said, "I told you. I found his body in the basement."

"Then what? You must have called someone," I guessed. "Who?"

She took a deep breath and let it out. "I suppose it doesn't matter anymore. I called Leo."

"I knew it. The tech lied for him." It all made sense. "He came here to help you get rid of the body while you sent a text from his phone so you'd have an alibi."

"I wasn't sure if Daniel was dead, so I told Leo he'd better bring something to knock him out, just in case. And while the rest of us were at Purrs and Pours, you showed up, so he used the sedative on you. I was furious when I found out he'd locked you in one of the storage rooms. How were we supposed to cover that up? To be honest, I was relieved when you escaped. I hoped no one would believe your story."

"I doubt anyone would have if Daniel's body hadn't washed ashore."

At a sound coming from above us, Jane picked up her shovel and resumed helping me dig.

Mrs. Nettle's voice came from above. "That's much better. Take a short break for dinner, then get back to work."

Two bottles of water landed near us, followed by a paper bag. I passed Jane one of the bottles and the bag, which smelled like burgers. I had no appetite.

"What are you going to do with us once we find the gold?" I asked.

"Oh, Jane's been blabbing, has she?" She sneered

down at me. "As soon as I have the treasure, I'll be packing up and leaving town. When I'm safe and sound, I'll make a call and let someone know where you are. I'm not a monster, you know."

"What about the cats?" I asked. "You're just going to abandon them?"

"I'm taking them with me. And when we get settled in our new town, I'll have enough money to rescue even more cats and spread the word that everyone should have at least one cat. Cats give you unconditional love."

There was one question she hadn't answered yet. "Was there ever really a Mr. Nettle, or did you make him up?"

Mrs. Nettle's face reddened. "Stop talking and dig." The trapdoor slammed shut.

Chapter Twenty-Five

Jane could hardly have looked more annoyed if she tried. "Good job pissing off Mrs. Nettle. What was the point of that?"

I only half listened to her complaining. My shovel had hit something hard. I jumped into the hole and got down on my hands and knees to scrape at the dirt.

"Did you find it?" Jane didn't try to hide her excitement. "Did you find the treasure?"

I'd found something. "It looks rusty."

She crawled over to have a look. "Is it a metal trunk? Can you open it?"

I stared at the rust-colored boulder I'd just uncovered. "It's a rock."

"That can't be... That must be..." She collapsed and began to sob, whether from disappointment or exhaustion, I couldn't tell.

"Sorry to tell you this, but I bet that thing is what triggered your metal detector. What's Mrs. Nettle going to do when she finds out there's no treasure, just a big rock?"

Jane didn't answer, but I had a pretty good idea. Most likely, she'd close the trapdoor and leave.

"Do you think you could give me a boost?"

She stopped crying long enough to say, "There's no way out. No hope."

"Fine. I'll do it on my own."

There had to be a way to climb out, but the closed trapdoor overhead presented the biggest obstacle. It didn't appear to be heavy, since Mrs. Nettle had little trouble with it. Still, unless I was standing on something solid, I wouldn't have enough leverage to push it open from underneath.

As I surveyed my surroundings again, I was reminded of a movie I'd worked on years earlier where I'd had to make my way along a pipe while hanging upside down. When a bad guy appeared out of nowhere, I'd kicked him in the face. It was a dummy—but still it was a fun stunt.

A thick pipe stretched across the low ceiling of the sub-basement. It was rusted and patches of grime clung to its surface, but it was solid enough, I hoped. My palms were clammy, so I wiped them against my jeans and steeled myself.

With a running start, I leaped, grabbing the pipe with both hands. Hanging upside down like a bat, I locked my legs around it and began to shimmy toward the trapdoor, my heart pounding in my ears.

Hand over hand, inch by inch, I dragged myself forward. The rust bit into my palms but I kept moving.

As I neared the trapdoor, my arms ached fiercely.

Sucking in a breath, I let my legs swing back and then forward as my boots struck the wooden hatch with a thud. It rattled but held firm.

I cursed under my breath, then swung my legs again kicking as hard as I could.

The trapdoor flew open, and a flood of light spilled into the sub-basement. I grabbed the edge of the opening, ignoring the splinters stabbing at my fingers. With one last burst of effort, I pulled myself up and rolled onto the dusty floor above, gulping the fresh air.

Jane's voice came from below. "Are you just going to leave me here?"

"Yeah, I figured you wouldn't want to make Mrs. Nettle mad." I didn't have much choice anyway, at least for the moment, and I didn't feel that bad about it. After all, it was her greed that got us both trapped down there in the first place.

I shut the trapdoor and looked for a hiding place, sure that Mrs. Nettle must have heard the noise, but there was no place to hide in the empty room.

Footsteps approached and I began to panic. As she entered, I ducked behind the door, hoping Mrs. Nettle wouldn't look behind it. I'd gotten the idea from an episode of *Murder, She Wrote* I'd watched with Bobbie. I hoped it worked in real life.

Barely daring to breathe, I watched and waited. Mrs. Nettle opened the trapdoor and leaned over to check on us, but she was about to find out that one of us was missing.

"I thought I heard a noise. Are you two okay in there?" she asked, a note of forced sweetness in her voice.

Before Jane could answer, I kicked Mrs. Nettle's round backside. She screamed, flailed her arms, and fell through the trapdoor landing with a thunk.

As Mrs. Nettle wailed, Jane called out to me. "You're not going to leave me down here with her, are you?"

I called to her, "I'm sure you two have a lot to talk about." Feeling almost giddy, I hurried up the stairs and burst into the bookshop main floor, a wave of relief washing over me in the familiar surroundings. I reached in my pocket for my phone, then wanted to kick myself. It was down with Jane where I'd tossed it on the ground.

As I headed for the front door, Herman suddenly appeared from behind a bookshelf. I nearly ran into him. "We're closed you know." He drew out each word as if he had all the time in the world.

"We need to call the police." My words came in a rush. "Jane and Mrs. Nettle are trapped in the basement." The concerned look he gave me made me add, "Jane's okay, and Mrs. Nettle can't hurt anyone now. Can I use your phone?"

"There's a land line right back here in the office."

I followed Herman as he slowly made his way to the back of the shop. "Can we hurry a bit, please?"

He opened a door and gestured for me to enter. "Ladies first."

Before I stepped inside, I stopped. Was this another trap?

"Um, why don't you go first?" I gave him a friendly smile, but that quickly faded when I saw what he held.

I recognized the Glock pointing at me, although I

wasn't sure if it was a 19 or a 22. Either one would kill me with a single bullet.

"Look." I forced my voice to stay casual. "This has been a really tough day, and I'm getting tired of trying to figure out who the bad guys are. Is the Society for Ancient Wisdom just a bunch of evildoer wannabes? If you ask me, you're all pathetic. There are easier ways to get rich other than digging for gold, you know."

"I don't care about gold. I care about the mission."

"The mission?"

"Daniel Holland was a threat. A threat that had to be eliminated."

"So... you killed Daniel?"

"He was going to expose our mission and blow my cover. And Jane's. I couldn't let that happen."

Now I was really confused. "Are you saying you're some sort of undercover spy, like CIA or something?"

"The KGB has infiltrated our government, our schools, even our churches. They're indoctrinating our children in unholy communist propaganda and teaching them to think everyone deserves a fair share. But some people are better than other people."

"People like... you?"

"Like Jane and the other members of the Society. People who are intelligent and can rule over those less worthy."

"Wait. I thought you didn't know about the Society." I stared at the gun pointed at my chest and wondered what else Jane had lied to us about. "I'm sorry about whatever happened to you, but..." My voice trailed off as I heard footsteps. I would have been happy to see just about anyone at that moment.

Herman kept the gun trained on me while watching over my shoulder to see who had arrived.

Marty took in the sight of us with barely a reaction. "Hello, Herman. What's going on?"

"She's gotten in the way one time too many."

I held my breath, wanting to scream at Marty to call the cops, but I wasn't entirely sure if he was on my side.

"Did you help Herman get rid of Daniel's body after he killed him?" I asked Marty. Who else was strong enough? Not Jane or Mrs. Nettle.

Marty's eyes widened ever so slightly. "Herman killed..." He closed his eyes and let out a breath. "Of course. Then the others covered up for him."

I wanted to trust Marty, but why wasn't he getting help? "Would you please call the police now?" I pleaded.

Herman's hand holding the gun began to shake. "You reach for your phone, and I shoot her."

"Herman." Marty's voice was soft and soothing. "If you do that it will ruin everything for us, don't you see? You'll blow your cover, and Jane's, and the rest of the Society. And anyway, Herman, you can't shoot her."

"Yes, I can. And I will."

"Let me have the gun." Marty coaxed.

As I held my breath, Marty slowly placed his hand on the gun. Didn't he care that one twitch of Herman's trigger finger and I'd be dead? He wrapped his hand around the gun and gently took it from Herman.

Marty shook his head. "You can't shoot her because I

took all the bullets out of your gun." He handed the Glock to me, pulled out his phone, and called for help.

Turning the gun over in my hand, I pressed the magazine release, and the clip slid out with a metallic click.

My voice wavered. "Marty?"

"Hold on," he said as he spoke to the dispatcher. Moments later, he disconnected the call. "The police and paramedics are on their way."

"Yeah, I suppose it's not all that important considering how things worked out," I said, staring at the staggered stack of brass casings inside. "But this gun was loaded."

Marty gasped.

Herman showed no surprise. "I reloaded it this morning when I saw someone had taken the bullets out."

Chapter Twenty-Six

Marty apologized over and over while we waited for the police.

"I'm so sorry, Whit. I had a bad feeling about Herman, and I knew he had a gun, so I went by the bookstore, found it in his storage closet, and took the bullets out. It never occurred to me... but it should have. I shouldn't have... You might have been..." He stopped talking briefly, unable to finish a sentence.

"We won't mention that part to Bobbie, okay?" I didn't want either of us to get a lecture, and it would be the lecture of the century.

"Oh... Bobbie. What am I going to say to Bobbie?"

"Nothing. Please, say nothing. I'll do all the talking, got it?"

"But—"

I stopped him from saying more the only way I could think of—by kissing him. I kept kissing him long enough for his breathing to slow. He wrapped his arms around my waist and pulled me closer.

When I came up for breath, I said, "There's something you should know about me. I'm kind of a hot mess."

He blinked. "Who told you that?"

It took a moment to come up with an answer to his question. "Life."

"Life?"

"Pretty much. And all the things people don't say, but I can tell that they're thinking. And all the times I think I'm doing the right thing, but it turns out wrong. And—"

He interrupted me. "Whit. You're not a hot mess. You're a work in progress."

"I am?"

"Yes. And people don't always like works in progress, especially the people who are in charge. They like people to be predictable and toe the line. But you don't change the world by following the rules."

"I'm not trying to change the world."

He smiled. "You don't have to try. It just happens a little at a time. If there were enough people taking a stand and making small changes, the whole world would be a much better place."

"I like the sound of that."

"Also, you solved a murder and uncovered a plot… of some sort." He scratched his head. "Have you figured it all out?"

Had I? "Sure. Jane was greedy. Herman thought he was protecting Jane and her mission. And Mrs. Nettle didn't like being taken advantage of."

Triple Shot

Bobbie and Rosa arrived in time to see Herman taken away in handcuffs. The paramedics were treating Jane and Mrs. Nettle in the basement. Jane was dehydrated, but otherwise fine, while Mrs. Nettle had sustained some injuries when I shoved her through the trapdoor.

As the paramedics rolled her gurney through the bookshop, I called out to her. "So sorry about your ankle, Mrs. Nettle. Hope your recovery is long and painful." She spat at me as she passed.

"Where's Kit?" I asked Bobbie.

"I took a chance and locked her in my room with her blanket, some food, and a bowl of water. And I put the nature channel on TV." She rubbed my arm and gave me a look of concern. "Why don't I take you home so you can rest? You've had quite an ordeal."

That was true, but I felt a surge of energy and a strong desire to celebrate being alive.

"Let's go out," I said. "Call Bernard and Kelvin. Oh, and Mitsy. Marty and I can catch you up on everything."

"Do you know all the details?" Bobbie asked.

"I'm pretty sure I've got all the puzzle pieces, and with everybody's help, we can paint a picture for everyone, right, Marty?"

He grinned and took my hand. "I bet we can. By the way, your metaphor could use some work."

I gave him a wink. "My metaphors are a work in progress."

Bobbie raised an eyebrow as if she didn't know exactly what was going on.

I asked Marty, "Where should we go?"

"How about the Gastro Gnome?"

I answered him with a groan. "Anyplace but the Gastro Gnome." The gnome-themed restaurant gave me the willies, and I'd been through quite enough torture for one day.

Unfortunately, the Gastro Gnome was the only place in town that could accommodate a group our size so late in the evening.

When we arrived, Rosa waited by the restaurant's front door and began asking questions the moment she saw us.

"We'll tell you everything as soon as everyone is here." I grabbed Marty's arm and hurried past the gnome statuettes. I didn't make eye contact with the host in her bright red cone-shaped hat while Bobbie asked for a table.

Shortly after we were seated, Mitsy and Kelvin arrived together, giving me another reason for celebrating. Once Bernard arrived and we'd ordered our food, I began explaining, with Marty, Bobbie, and Bernard filling in gaps.

"It all started when Daniel Holland, a CIA operative who'd been selling classified information to the highest bidder, faked his death in 2007 by setting his house on fire, leaving someone inside so they'd find a dead body. I hope it was somebody who was already dead, but I suppose when they go back and do DNA testing, they'll be able to identify him."

"Didn't they have DNA testing in 2007?" Rosa asked.

"Let her tell her story," Bobbie chided her.

"No, that's a valid question. They would have checked

dental records, which no doubt were switched. When those were a match, there wouldn't have been any reason to test further, right Bernard?"

He nodded. "I was able to confirm that the accident that caused Jane's injuries happened in 2007. She happened to be inside when his ammunition stockpile exploded. Jane, or I should say Marnie, never walked again."

"I knew it!" Kelvin gave a triumphant fist pump. "I told you she was a spy."

"Yes," I admitted. "Technically, but she and Eleanor had desk jobs. I'm guessing Jane—I'm just going to keep calling her that to avoid confusion, if that's alright with you, Kelvin." He didn't object, so I continued. "Jane had some sort of dealings with agents, processing their expense accounts or making travel reservations or something like that. Or she might have had a more active role, but whatever she did isn't important now. At some point in time, she came into contact with Daniel and Herman."

"Herman?" Bobbie blurted out. "Is there anyone connected to that bookshop that wasn't a spy?" She glanced over at Marty, who raised his hand and said, "Me. Not a spy."

"Thank goodness for that," Bobbie said with obvious relief.

"I'm confused," Rosa said. "I still don't know who killed Daniel or attacked Whitley."

"Herman killed Daniel," I said. "He was fiercely loyal to Jane, so when he thought Daniel was a threat to her, he eliminated him, just as he'd been trained to do. He either didn't know or didn't care about the gold."

"What gold?" Rosa asked.

Mitsy spoke up. "My great-great-grandfather's gold. There's been a legend practically forever that Franklin Norvelt had buried his gold somewhere in town. Jane obviously thought it was under the bookshop. That was Norvelt's official home, where his wife and kids lived. But he spent most of his time with my great-great grandmother and their children at Chambers House."

Rosa furrowed her brow. "So, Jane heard about the legend that there was buried treasure and bought the bookshop thinking that's where it must have been buried?"

"Exactly," I said. "Herman's lived in Arrow Springs for years and must have told her about the legend. Jane had left the CIA and was at loose ends, so running a bookstore and digging for gold must have sounded like an adventure."

Rosa lifted her hand tentatively. "I don't want to interrupt, but am I the only one wondering if there really is gold buried under the bookshop?"

"Jane certainly thought so, otherwise we wouldn't have been digging down there, but there was only rock with a high metal content that triggered her industrial strength metal detector." I rubbed my palms. "I have blisters on my hands from digging." I held out my hands for the others to see. "Luckily, I didn't get any splinters. The handle wasn't wood like the other shovel's..." What other shovel?

I'd seen a dirty shovel in a closet somewhere. A broom, a shovel, and a vacuum cleaner at the... "At the Chambers house. The shovel was in a closet right by..." I nudged Marty to let me out of the booth.

"Right by what?" he asked.

"By the stairs to the basement." I slid out of the booth and tapped Mitsy on the shoulder. "Your great-great grandmother Destiny lived there, right? And Franklin Norvelt trusted her with the location of his remaining wealth. What if it's buried under Chambers House?"

She was out of her seat before I finished talking. Bobbie pulled out her credit card and waved the server over.

Marty caught up with me as I stepped out the front door of the Gastro Gnome into the dark night. As soon as I got my bearings, I speed walked across Main Street, then took off at a run.

Was there any rush? Probably not, but I needed to do something with the excess adrenaline pumping through my veins.

The Chambers House was a few blocks on the other side of the square, and I hadn't even broken a sweat by the time I passed the microbrewery. As I approached the old house, I spotted a car in the darkened parking lot on the right side of the house. No one appeared to be in it.

I crept up the front steps to the door and tried the handle, not at all surprised to find it locked. As I began looking for another way in, Marty showed up, panting heavily.

"Do you recognize the sedan in the parking lot?" I asked.

He struggled to catch his breath. "Should I?"

While he took a closer look, I checked the first-floor windows, starting with the ones in front and working my way along the side. By the time I'd returned to the front porch, Mitsy and Kelvin arrived together.

I joined them on the sidewalk and peered at the house. My eyes were adjusting to the darkness, but I couldn't tell if there were any lights on inside. "The door is locked. I guess I'll have to find a way to climb up to the second floor and hope a window is open."

"Or..." Mitsy reached into her pocket. "You could use the keys."

I grinned. "You're the best. I'll go in, and you three can stay out of sight and keep watch."

Mitsy unlocked the front door and pushed it open. "The guys can wait outside. I'm going with you."

I hesitated. "But Mitsy," I whispered, "it could be dangerous."

She blocked the doorway, one hand on each jamb. "If you're going, I'm going."

Not waiting for my answer, she stepped inside the pitch-black parlor. I followed close behind, turning on my phone's flashlight app.

We made our way around the furniture into the next room. When we reached the door to the basement, my heart skipped a beat.

A sliver of light shone through the bottom of the basement door.

Chapter Twenty-Seven

I held a finger to my mouth and whispered, "I think someone's here."

"Now what?" Mitsy whispered back.

That was a good question. Maybe it would have been best to make a plan before I went running off, but excitement had gotten the better of me. I gestured for her to follow me back to the front door.

"Let's get out of here and find somewhere safe to call the police." I didn't like putting Mitsy in danger. She seemed so small and vulnerable.

"I'm not going anywhere," Mitsy said. "This is my family's house."

"But what if..." My voice trailed off, but we could both imagine the what ifs.

"What if they have a gun?" Mitsy reached under her jacket and pulled out a pistol. "I came prepared."

Mitsy having a gun didn't exactly reassure me, but I

kept that to myself. As I pondered our choices, a sound came from the back of the house.

"What was that?" she whispered, but I was already halfway to the back door. As I stood in the dark parlor and listened, I heard someone close the back door and lock it, then the screen door shut softly. Within seconds, I was at the back door. I unlocked it and stepped down the back stairs, the screen door slamming behind me. The moon emerged for a moment, just long enough to illuminate the wide eyes of the person putting a box into her trunk.

Eleanor Thorne slammed the trunk and got in her car.

I launched into a full sprint as Eleanor's car lurched backward out of the parking space. As she sped toward the exit, I threw myself onto the hood. My body hit the cold metal with a thud nearly knocking the breath out of me.

Eleanor's eyes widened for a split second before narrowing into a furious glare. She floored the accelerator, and the sudden jolt sent me sprawling against the windshield. My cheek pressed against the glass as I grabbed hold of the windshield wipers. She took a sharp turn onto the street, nearly knocking me off the hood. As she jerked the steering wheel one way and then the other, doing her best to dislodge me, I held on.

Another violent jerk of the wheel sent my legs sliding, and every muscle screamed as I fought to stay on. No way was I letting her get away.

Three gunshots cracked through the air, one after the other. My heart pounded as I flattened my body against the hood and braced for the worst. Who thought that firing at a moving car was a good idea?

The car lurched violently, swerving more erratically

than before. A hollow thump, thump, thump, was followed by the grinding squeal of the rim scraping on the road. We went into a spin, and the sickening crunch of metal colliding with metal rang out as the car slammed into a parked vehicle.

Eleanor flung the driver's door open, and she bolted down the sidewalk, surprisingly fast for her age. I was faster. Within moments, I caught up with her and tackled her. We hit the concrete hard, and I pinned her down as she twisted and thrashed beneath me.

"That must have hurt," I said. "Good." I knelt on her back as I pulled the belt from my jeans and wrapped it tightly around her wrists.

Only then did I see why the car had spun out of control. Two flat tires.

As I kept her pinned down under my knees, I pressed my hands together to stem the bleeding from my scraped palms.

Marty jogged over to us and crouched down next to me as sirens began to wail in the distance. He took my hands in his, inspecting my palms.

"You weren't going to let go for anything, were you?" He pulled his sweater over his head, then the t-shirt underneath.

The sight of his toned chest made me forget my injuries for a moment. "Do you really think this is the time or the place?"

He chuckled as he put his sweater back on and gently wrapped the t-shirt around my hands. "Maybe not, but sometimes, in the heat of the battle, it's easy to get carried away."

Before I could respond, his lips were on mine. I closed my eyes and almost forgot where I was. Almost.

Eleanor squirmed under my knee. "You're hurting me."

Marty ended the kiss. "We'll pick up where we left off later."

"Not too much later I hope?" I asked. "Would you sit on her for a bit?"

"Gladly."

Bobbie scurried over and threw her arms around me. "What were you thinking, running off like that?"

As she squeezed me tightly, I managed to say, "I probably wasn't thinking."

"Nothing new, I suppose," she grumbled.

I went over to Eleanor's car and found the trunk release. Inside were boxes of books.

Mitsy hovered next to me. "All that for some books?"

"I doubt it." I gave her a grin as Bobbie hurried over. I pulled out book after book, tossing them aside, until I uncovered a layer of gold bars. "There's Norvelt's gold."

Bobbie gasped. "There really was a treasure."

Mitsy looked from her to me. "There always was a treasure. This town and the people in it are worth so much more than gold bars."

The police had plenty of questions considering it was their second call of the day where I was involved. A busy day for the Arrow Springs Police Department.

I answered Deputy Wallenthorp's questions while one of the paramedics bandaged my hands. I had questions of my own, like who had shot out the tires of Eleanor's car. If it was Mitsy, as I suspected, she was an amazing shot.

Chapter Twenty-Eight

The next morning, the kitchen was empty, but the coffeepot was full, so I poured myself a cup and went looking for Bobbie. Kit followed me through the living room, biting at the heels of my slippers.

"If you make me fall and break an ankle, no more treats for the next ten years," I warned, shaking my foot to shoo her away.

The crisp morning air greeted me as I slid open the door to the deck. Kit darted between my legs, her nails skittering on the wood as she raced past Bobbie and headed for the railing.

"Don't you even think about it," I scolded sharply.

Kit froze, her head low, a guttural growl rising from her throat.

"You ungrateful mutt. Are you growling at me?"

"We have a visitor," Bobbie said from her perch at the patio table.

I followed her gaze and stopped short. A woman stood at the other side of the deck, framed by the backdrop of the pine forest, her wavy auburn hair glowing in the early morning sunlight. As she took off her dark glasses, her vibrant blue eyes, the exact same shade as Bobbie's, fixed on me with unsettling intensity.

My mouth had gone dry. "Hello, Julia."

"Hello, Whitley." Julia smiled and for a moment, the world stood still. Birds chirped in the distance, a sunbeam painted the deck in golden light, and a soft wind caressed my cheek.

Before I could process the weight of her presence, she said, "You're even more beautiful in person than you are in your pictures."

"Me?" I snorted, breaking the spell. "I'm not beautiful. I was never beautiful." Not compared to Julia with her radiant complexion, flawless features, and high cheekbones. "At least I got your cheekbones."

Julia's smile widened. "You have Alejandro's eyes. I always told him I would kill for those eyelashes. And here it turns out you got them."

"I had to learn martial arts just to protect myself. They go for a pretty penny on the eyelash black market."

Julia turned her gaze to Bobbie. "You were right about her sass. I can only imagine what she was like as a teenager."

Before I could stop myself, I blurted out, "Yeah, you wouldn't know because you weren't around."

Her smile faded. "If you knew how hard it was to stay away..."

"Oh, really?" I snapped as the floodgates opened. "You know these days they have all kinds of modern inventions like phones and computers. You can even video chat with people who are thousands of miles away. If, you know, you really wanted to."

"Whitley," Bobbie said. "You don't know the whole story."

"You never gave her...?" Julia didn't finish her question.

I plopped down onto one of the Adirondack chairs, the hard wood pressing against my back. "You're right. I don't know the whole story. And why not? I'm thirty years old. I'm not a child anymore."

"You deserve the truth." Julia joined Bobbie at the patio table. "And the truth is that since the day you were born, I have done everything I could to keep you safe by making sure that they didn't find out about you."

"They? You mean like Isabella."

"Isabella, yes. But most of all, Isabella and Alejandro's father, Don Carlos. There are no limits to what he would do to get back at Alejandro and me." She lowered her eyes. "Especially me. He believes I turned his son against him."

"You could have taken me with you." Bitterness cut through my voice like glass. "Or you could have left him and kept me." I asked the question I'd wanted an answer for since I was a child. "Why did you choose him over me?"

Her smile returned, but it was tinged with sadness. "We'd already made a deal to give evidence to extradite Don Carlos to the U.S. when I found out I was pregnant.

Your existence had to be kept a secret, or he would have used you to get to me. I always planned to come back after he was put in jail, but that day never came. He had too much power and money, and there were too many corrupt officials happy to take bribes."

"You could have taken me with you into witness protection."

Her eyes widened. "I couldn't do that to you—never being able to tell anyone who you really are, never feeling safe. I chose that life, and not a day goes by that I don't wonder if I made the right decision."

I wanted to cry, scream, or hurl a chair off the deck, but I didn't want her to see how much she'd hurt me. Clenching my jaw, I asked, "Okay, so what are you doing here now? I'm guessing this isn't a family reunion."

"I wish," she said in a voice so soft I barely heard.

Bobbie reached out and took her hand, and the two of them shared a sweet mother-daughter moment. It pissed me off.

"Well?" My impatience came through in my voice, but I didn't care.

Julia turned to me, her face an unreadable mask. "Now that Isabella knows about you, it's only a matter a time before Don Carlos tracks you down. When I shot at her limo—"

"That was you?"

She nodded. "I considered aiming at her skull. That would have put an end to it."

Bobbie spoke up. "There must be less drastic measures we can take. Is there no way to reason with her?"

Julia laughed without humor. "Isabella will try her

best to convince Whitley to go with her. If she can't manage that, I have no doubt she'll tell him how to find his granddaughter."

"How do we know she hasn't told him about me already?" I asked.

"Isabella has a pathological need to impress her father, since, to him, women are important only for having babies. She'll want to make a dramatic entrance and present him with his granddaughter so she can get all the glory. Telling him about you will be her backup plan, and unless my sister-in-law is dead, I don't see how to keep her from talking."

An idea brewed in my mind. "There is another way she would leave us alone."

"Yes?" Bobbie's voice wavered.

I looked from Bobbie to Julia. "If *I* were dead."

Bobbie gasped, and she pushed herself up from her chair. "What hairbrained scheme have you come up with now?"

"Don't worry, Bobbie." I gave her my calmest smile. "I have no plans to die."

"Thank goodness for that." She sat back down, muttering something under her breath.

I picked up our mugs. "I'll refill our coffee, and we can talk more." I gave Julia a look, hoping she'd follow me. She got the hint and told Bobbie she'd be right back.

In the kitchen, alone with her, all my emotions came to the surface. I struggled to hold back tears, though I couldn't have said if they were sad, angry, or some other feeling I'd yet to identify.

Julia softly asked, "Can I at least have one hug?"

As the sight of her outstretched arms, my resolve faltered, and I fell into her embrace. As she wrapped her arms around me, I let go of the pain I felt for being abandoned. Tears flowed, and I didn't try to stop them. I held onto her, feeling her warm breath and breathing in her somehow familiar scent.

When I pulled away, I saw she'd been crying too. I grabbed some napkins from the counter, handing her one before wiping the tears from my face.

"I'm not usually a crier. I'm more of a 'kick-ass first and ask questions later' kind of person." I blew my nose. "Speaking of kicking ass, I wouldn't mind going one-on-one with Isabella. But that's not going to solve this problem."

Julia eyed me with curiosity. "You have a plan, don't you?"

"Oh, boy, do I. Bobbie's not going to like it, so I need a diversion."

"Like a commotion of some kind?"

"Sort of. Her name is Rosa." I didn't have time to explain more. "I'll call Isabella and see if she'll meet me somewhere this morning."

Isabella sounded pleased to hear from me. The airport had reopened, and she was set to fly to San Diego that morning, unsure when she'd be back. I might have implied I'd go with her.

Twenty minutes later, I had everything I needed in a duffle bag ready to go. Five minutes after that, three heavy bangs rattled the door. I opened it and Rosa burst through.

She frantically cried out, "Where's Bobbie?"

"Out on the deck."

"Oh, thank goodness! You'll never believe what happened."

I gave Rosa a thumbs-up. She smiled briefly before resuming her performance. Turning to Julia, I said, "Let's get out of here before Bobbie notices we're missing."

Chapter Twenty-Nine

The road twisted through the forest before leveling out as my car approached the airport. I followed Isabella's instructions, pulling up to a private hangar.

I parked the car and stepped out, questioning my own sanity. Was this plan as ridiculous as it felt? "Too late now," I muttered, walking toward the yawning open doors of the hangar. The jet loomed large, its sleek lines glowing under the harsh overhead lights. The space was eerily quiet and smelled of jet fuel and stale oil.

"Isabella?" My voice echoed in the cavernous space.

I turned at the sound of heels clicking on the concrete floor. Isabella appeared at the far end of the hangar. She looked so small, so harmless, I felt my shoulders relax.

Don't let your guard down, Julia's voice echoed in my head. *She'd kill her own brother to get what she wants.*

What did she want? Was this all to earn Daddy's love? Or maybe evil was in her DNA. If so, did I have an evil gene too? It might explain a few things. On the other hand, maybe Isabella was just a spoiled, broken child in a grown woman's body.

But broken or not, she was dangerous.

Isabella came within a few feet of where I stood next to the jet and stopped.

"Hello, Whitley." She wore all black with a camel-colored cashmere coat draped over her shoulders. "Is your bag in the car?"

"I've given it some more thought, and I've decided it wouldn't be in my best interests to come with you."

Her dark eyes, so like mine, turned cold as if she'd flicked off the light. "What makes you think I care about your best interests?"

The truth was out. Good. No need to have any reservations about what came next. "I know all about my grandfather. Once you take me to him, he'll use me to get to Julia and Alejandro."

She didn't appear surprised at how much I'd learned since we last talked. With a smile that oozed with fake sincerity, she said, "Perhaps he simply wants to meet his granddaughter."

I snickered. "Yeah. Maybe he'll invite me to join the family business. I could be one of your mules, sneaking contraband over the border. Does it pay well?"

She folded her arms over her chest. "Are you coming with me or not?"

"That would be not."

Her voice turned to ice. "Bruno!"

A dark-haired man nearly as wide as he was tall

emerged from the jet. He lumbered down the steps with deliberate slowness.

The man was straight out of central casting. About five foot eight and at least two hundred and fifty pounds, with a pockmarked face and a scar over his right eye. His nose looked like it had been broken more than once.

I held up my hands to stop him from coming closer. "No need to get physical, dude."

He stood a foot or so away from me, his dark eyes boring into me as he waited for instructions from Isabella. I had a bad feeling I knew what those instructions would be.

"Teach her some manners," Isabella said, her voice soft but cutting.

At her command, Bruno lunged.

I stepped aside, narrowly dodging the meaty hand that reached for my arm. He moved faster than I expected, swinging a punch at my head. I ducked, feeling the rush of air as his fist grazed my hair.

"Easy there!" I said, feinting to the right before pivoting left.

He growled, turning toward me with surprising agility. I darted backward, but he grabbed the front of my favorite sweatshirt, tearing a hole in the seam.

"Okay, now it's personal," I muttered, twisting in his grip.

With all the force I could muster, I drove my knee into his stomach. Okay, it might have been a little lower than his stomach, but this wasn't the time to fight fair. He grunted and doubled over as I twisted free.

"Enough!" Isabella called out.

When I saw she had a gun pointed at me, I took a step back and raised my arms in surrender. "What's with everyone and their guns lately? Was there a 'buy two, get one free' deal I missed out on?"

"Very funny." Her voice, cold as ice, sent a shiver down my back. "I'm done playing games. Get on the plane."

"Or what?" I asked, though I was pretty sure I knew the answer. "You're going to shoot me?"

"Don't think I won't." Something about the defiant way she held her chin made me believe her.

I kept my voice steady—not an easy task at that moment. "What will your daddy have to say about that?"

Isabella's grip on the gun didn't falter, but the corner of her mouth twitched. "Who's going to tell him?"

Julia's voice rang out from the hangar opening. "I will." She stood silhouetted against the harsh morning light, holding a pistol pointed at Isabella.

"Hello, Julia." Isabella tried to mask her surprise. "Your daughter is a smart one. She thinks Daddy won't be happy if I shoot her. I suppose she's right." She slowly moved her gun until it was aimed at Julia. "But he'll throw me a party if I bring home your dead body."

Julia tilted her head slightly, her gun shifting until it was pointed directly at my chest. "If Don Carlos finds out that you're responsible for the death of his favorite son's child, you'll be thrown out on the street with nothing."

Isabella's mouth parted as her composure began to crack. "You wouldn't kill your own child."

"I would do anything to keep me and Alejandro safe from your father."

"What would Alejandro say?" Isabella's voice was strident, almost panicky. "He'll never forgive you."

A smile slowly formed on Julia's face. "Whitley isn't Alejandro's daughter, but that doesn't mean your father won't use her to get to us. To me."

"But she's your daughter."

"True, but..." Julia paused dramatically, then shrugged. "I barely know the girl."

Julia fired three times.

The sound was deafening and someone screamed. It might have been me as I staggered backward clutching my chest. Warm liquid oozed between my fingers as I hit the ground hard, my head slamming against the cement floor.

And then everything went black.

Chapter Thirty

By the time I came to, chaos had unfolded around me. I lay still, barely daring to breathe. I'd had plenty of practice playing dead on movie sets, but this was for real. Isabella had to believe it was real.

Footsteps approached me. Not Isabella's heels, but Julia's flats. She reached down and tugged at my hair.

Her voice sounded far away. "Here you go. A DNA sample for you to test in case you don't believe me. Your brother really is a good man. He offered to marry me knowing the baby wasn't his." Sirens sounded in the distance. "You might want to get out of here before the cops come."

Isabella began screaming at everyone. The jet's engine came to life with a deafening roar and after what felt like an eternity, it slowly taxied out of the hangar and onto the jetway.

Still, I remained motionless, not daring to open my eyes.

"Whitley!" Julia's voice, sharp and panicked, broke through the fading noise.

I cracked one eye open. "Is the coast clear?"

"Oh, thank goodness you're all right." She knelt beside me, her face breaking into a grin. "We did it! You should have seen Isabella's face. She completely freaked out."

"That's great." Sitting up slowly, I held onto my head with both hands and groaned. "On set, there's always a soft landing. I should have thought of that. Next time I'm going to strap a pillow onto the back of my head."

"Next time? Let's hope there's no 'next time'." She gently probed the back of my skull, where a knot would already be forming. "Let's go home and get you some ice. I hope you brought a change of clothes," she said as she helped me get to my feet. "Bobbie will have a heart attack if she sees you with blood all over your shirt."

"Bobbie may have friends in high places, but I have friends with fake blood."

"And prop guns."

I reached out to take the gun from her. "I had a feeling it might come in handy one day."

Chapter Thirty-One

The sun dipped low over the pine-covered mountains, casting golden light across the deck. I sat with my feet propped up, wrapped in a blanket far too heavy for the mild spring air. Julia had insisted on tucking it around my shoulders, treating me like a porcelain doll. Bobbie hovered nearby, bringing food and drinks until the table next to me was cluttered with a teapot, a cup of tea, a water bottle, and a plate of half-eaten cookies.

"You're smothering me." I didn't mind, of course, but it was in my nature to complain.

"It's not every day you get shot at by your own mother." Julia fluffed the pillow under my head. "Besides, I like taking care of you. It hardly makes up for..." Her voice trailed off.

I reached out and squeezed her hand. My headache had begun to fade, but the lump, still tender, would take days to subside. After a week of near-death experiences and family drama that could fill an entire season of TV, I felt at home for the first time in a very long time. Maybe the first time ever.

The front doorbell rang, and a bark came from under the blanket. After a lot of squirming, Kit poked her head out while Bobbie pushed herself up with a groan, mumbling about unannounced visitors.

Julia topped off my tea and handed me the cup, saying, "You need to stay hydrated."

"Yes, Mom." The word sounded strange to my ears, not surprising considering it was the first time I'd called her that. A twinge of guilt jabbed at me, and I felt the need to defend the woman who'd raised me. "Angela was good to me."

"I know. If she hadn't been, I would have come back and taken you away. I know she wasn't perfect, but she did try her best, according to Bobbie anyway."

I nodded. "I don't think being a mom came naturally to her." I could have told her all the ways that Angela had failed me as a mother, but what was the point? "But no one's mother is perfect, right? I mean, I love Bobbie to pieces, but I bet she had her moments."

Julia chuckled. "*We* had our moments. I wasn't an easy kid, especially as a teenager. We had these huge fights, with me yelling and slamming doors. Then I met Alejandro, and one day after a big blowout with Bobbie, I took off with him and never came back."

Bobbie reappeared in the doorway. "And I never forgave myself."

Julia went to her, and they hugged for a long time, as if

trying to make up for all the missed hugs over the past several decades.

When they let each other go, Bobbie dabbed at her eyes. "But you did come back. To have your baby."

Julia returned to her seat next to me and fussed with my blanket. "I couldn't let Alejandro's family know about the baby. It's a miracle that we kept it a secret for thirty years."

"And maybe it will be a secret for even longer," I said. "Assuming that Isabella doesn't figure out that we switched the hair sample. Whose hair did you give her, anyway?"

"Bobbie's. I raided her hairbrush and found some strands that weren't gray. I wanted hair from a relative of mine, in case she really did have it tested."

I leaned back into the sea of cushions Bobbie had stacked on the chair, just the way I liked them.

"Who was at the door?" I asked Bobbie.

"A delivery for you." She stepped back into the house and reappeared with a terra cotta pot planted with what looked like a stick with needles. It stood about a foot and a half tall. "There's no card. Any guess who sent it?"

I took the scraggly thing from her and read the plastic label stuck in the dirt. "It's a Ponderosa Pine from the Arrow Springs Conservancy." I read the next line to myself. "The Legacy Pines Initiative propagates saplings from the oldest and most iconic trees in Arrow Springs and surrounding areas."

I fought back the tears welling up. "It's from Marty."

"I don't understand people these days," Bobbie muttered. "What's wrong with sending a nice bouquet?"

"Or a casserole," I said. "I keep waiting for someone to show up with one like they did in the old days."

Bobbie chuckled. "There's one in the fridge. Rosa brought it when she came by to check on you earlier."

"Awesome." I turned to Julia. "Are you staying for dinner?"

"I'd like that," Julia said with a hesitant smile. "But I'll have to leave in the morning."

"So soon?" When her smile disappeared, I changed my tune. "That's okay. We can do a lot of catching up in one night, but I hope you don't plan on getting much sleep."

"She's not kidding," Bobbie said. "She'll talk all night if you let her."

Julia stood. "First, I have something I want you to see." She went into the house, returning shortly with a cookie tin. She handed it to me.

"What is this?" I asked. "Sewing supplies? If you need a button sewn on or something, I'm not the one you should ask."

Bobbie got to her feet faster than I'd seen her move in a long time. "Where did you get that?" Before Julia could answer, she said, "You have no business going through my closets."

Anger seeped into Julia's voice. "I have every business." She reached for Bobbie's hand. "Mom, it's time she knew."

"Knew what?" I asked.

"Just open the tin."

I pried the lid off. Inside was a stack of letters—letters

addressed to me, sent to Bobbie's address, and stuffed, unopened, into this tin.

Not daring to look at Bobbie or Julia, I carefully took a letter from top of the pile and opened it.

My darling Whitley,

Happy birthday! I hope you are happy, and although I know it's selfish, my heart is breaking knowing that we have been apart for thirty years. Thirty years!

Not a day has passed without me thinking of you and sending you my love.

I couldn't read the rest through my tears. "You wrote to me."

"Of course I did," Julia said, her voice barely more than a whisper.

I couldn't look at Bobbie. Someday I'd forgive her for keeping these letters from me, but that would have to wait.

As I took in Julia's adoring gaze, all the terrible things I'd believed about myself melted away. In that moment, I understood everything. I was wanted. I belonged. I was loved.

"No matter what happens..." I couldn't finish the words.

"No matter what happens or where I go," Julia said, beaming, "I will be a part of your life now and forever."

Chapter Thirty-Two

Spring arrived late, making up for its tardiness by bringing along a heat wave. I practically skipped down the hall to the kitchen, with Kit prancing around me.

Bobbie set down her coffee mug. "You seem cheerful this morning."

"It's going to be seventy-two degrees today and sunny. I can wear shorts. Do you know how long it's been since I've worn a pair of shorts?" I paused, trying to remember. "My legs must be extra pale."

"They'll never be as pale as these." Bobbie pulled up a pant leg, displaying a lily-white calf.

"No, stop! You're blinding me!" I teased.

"Is it possible you're also excited about Birch Street Books' grand re-opening?" Bobbie asked.

"With Marty as the owner, I'm hoping he'll help me get over the cringy memories I have of the place. We're going to completely redo the basement to make it cozy and welcoming."

"We?" Bobbie raised her eyebrows meaningfully.

"I'm his first employee," I said casually, not at all sure why I was so excited. "It's just a part-time, minimum-wage job, and probably temporary, but Marty promised to work around my coaching schedule at the gymnastics center when summer comes."

"I can't wait to hear all the stories you come home with about the preteen girls."

"Stories?" I wasn't planning to get involved in their drama. "I'm teaching them gymnastics techniques, not hanging out with them."

Bobbie nodded knowingly. "I don't want to bring up a sensitive subject, but have you decided to step back from your stunt career?"

I'd been waiting for that question for weeks and wasn't sure how I'd answer it when the time came. Now I knew exactly what to say.

"Here's the thing." I sat down at the table across from her. "I was hoping you'd let me stay with you a while longer."

"A while?" One corner of her mouth twitched. "How long were you thinking?"

I tapped my chin, pretending to be thinking it over. "Maybe a few years?" I shrugged. "I don't know. Maybe forever. Or until you get tired of me."

She squawked a laugh and threw her hand across her mouth.

"What's so funny?" I asked, not sure if I should be offended.

"Get tired of you, Whitley Leland? The most unpredictable, clever, and adventurous person I've ever met? Not a chance. You can stay here as long as you want."

"Thanks, Bobbie," I murmured, as she wrapped me in a hug.

She whispered in my ear, "Don't think it's a free ride. I'm going to need your help at Arrow Investigations more now than ever."

I pulled back. "Why is that?"

"I've completed my coursework, and Bernard has made me lead investigator on our next case."

"Our next case? We have a case?"

Bobbie gave me a sly grin. "We certainly do. Sit down and I'll tell you all about it."

Thank you for reading *Triple Shot, A Last Call Crime Club Mystery*.

Sign up for updates at kcwalkerauthor.com.

Want more?

KC Walker also writes and publishes sweet cozy mysteries under the name Karen Sue Walker. You can find her Bridal Shop Mysteries and Haunted Tearoom Mysteries on Amazon. Visit karensuewalker.com to learn more.

By the way, I love hearing from readers—you can email me at kc@karensuewalker.com.